HOMESCHOOL HUNTLEY'S FIRST TRUE ROMANCE

VANESSA GRAY BARTAL

DRY CREEK PRESS

AUTHOR'S NOTE

I try hard to keep all of my books clean and wholesome, sweet and cozy, especially young adult fiction. However, occasionally a book deals with complex material, (although hopefully in a safe and positive manner.) This book tackles a couple of topics that sensitive readers may find triggering, including abuse and mental health. For especially young or sensitive readers, a parental preview may be in order.

Thank you,

Joy Mae Boone.

CHAPTER 1

"I'm not going to need that," I said.

"You might," my twin sister, Haven, said as she carefully rolled the tie and tucked it in my suitcase.

"Haven, it's weather camp. In what universe would that require a tie?"

"In the universe where you might go on a date." Stubbornly, she gave the tie a little pat and regarded me, daring me to disagree again. Of course I wouldn't. I was more than happy for Haven to arrange my suitcase, my life, and anything else she wanted. The fact that I only had a few weeks left before she moved nine hours away for college loomed heavy in both our hearts. Worse, I would be spending most of that time away from her while I was the one at camp for once.

Haven sank to my bed, tucking her feet beneath her. "I'm going to miss you."

I sat down beside her. "I'm going to miss you, too." She leaned on me, resting her head on my shoulder. Every memory from my entire life was entwined with Haven. And now all of a sudden it felt like we were about to diverge. After this year, things would never be the same again.

I slipped my arm around her and gave her a sideways hug. "It's not easy to be the one left behind, huh?"

She shook her head and dashed at her eyes.

"It's only for a couple of weeks," I said, but it wasn't. It was the beginning of the end, and we both felt it.

Haven hugged me hard, pressing her face to my shoulder. "Have fun. Be good."

I returned her hug, chuckling. "You're telling me to be good?"

She eased back and peered into my face, eyes serious. "Yes. You've never been away from home before. There will be a lot of new temptations. Don't fall for any of them. Be the same strong Huntley I know and love."

"I promise," I said.

She gave me a watery smile and patted my cheek. "Ready?"

My chest fluttered with nerves. I tamped them down. I was almost eighteen years old. I could survive a few weeks away from my mommy and daddy and siblings.

"Yes." I stood and shouldered my bag. Haven tucked her hand in mine, a sign of her impending dread over my departure. The worse she felt, the more affectionate she was. We walked down the stairs and encountered my other best friend, Haven's boyfriend, Sutton. His eyes glanced worriedly at Haven before landing on me with a smile.

"Ready?" he asked.

"Definitively," I said with more resolve than I'd used with Haven.

Sutton rolled his eyes. "You sound like your sister."

"You mean he sounds smart," Haven said. She let go of me to stand by him. There was probably a metaphor in there if I cared to look for it. Sutton eased his arm around her and gave her a squeeze.

"Take good care of her," I said, and it wasn't figurative. Sutton had taken over my job. Now he and Haven worked together every day at our dad's car washes, transporting large sums of money. Leaving Haven unprotected had been my biggest argument against camp until Sutton stepped forward and offered to do her rounds with her.

"I will," Sutton agreed solemnly.

"Guys, I'm right here. You could at least pretend we live in the twenty first century," Haven complained.

"Shh, baby, the men are talking," Sutton said.

It wasn't the sort of comment I could get away with, but it was the sort I could laugh at, especially when Haven launched herself at his back and bit his neck, forcing him to convulse in a fit of giggles.

"Uncle," Sutton gasped. He was ridiculously ticklish, a secret he guarded closely. I wondered what our friends at school would say if they could see him now. He only dropped the cool guy persona when he was with us. I liked him better without it. The two of them seemed to remember me at the same moment, their smiles slipping as they faced me.

Haven stepped forward and gave me a tight hug. She shuddered but managed to press back the tears. "Have so much fun. I love you."

"I love you, too." I squeezed her as tightly as I dared, always cognizant of her tiny size. I let her go and bumped fists with Sutton, who looked relieved. He wasn't a hugger, except with Haven, of course. I gave him a reprieve for now, but later, when he left for college, I'd hug him. And probably cry, too.

My parents were letting me drive myself to camp. It was a huge leap of trust and independence, almost like being at college. Haven had been a little bitter because she wasn't allowed to take the car next year or drive herself to or from school. But Sutton would only be twenty five minutes away from her, and my parents would likely give him gas money to drive her places.

The first half of camp was three hours away. Later, we'd move to a more remote location for some hands-on activities. As much as I would miss my family, I was excited to be around other people who were as into the weather as I was. Atmosphere geeks, as Haven lovingly called us.

The only drawback to the plan was Bellamy Brown, a childhood friend from my homeschool days who was also going to camp. I was her ride now, too. Don't get me wrong, Bellamy was okay. It's just… There are different homeschool families. To the outside observer, we probably all look the same, lots of people, lots of chaos. But in actuality my mom was like a submarine commander. Yes, there were a lot of us, but each had an assigned space and job. We worked as a cohesive and organized unit. And then there were families like Bellamy's. She had seven siblings who always seemed to be going twelve different directions. They wore whatever they found, routinely went without combing their hair or washing their faces. Their mother was a space cadet who never seemed to know where she was or what she was doing, and Bellamy wasn't far behind. I'd known her forever, for as long as I could remember, yet we'd never been close. Something about her bugged me, if I'm being honest. Maybe it was because she never seemed to take anything seriously. Maybe it was because she called me Homeschool Huntley until last year when I transferred to public school and she began calling me High School Huntley. What would she call me now, Graduate Huntley? I was about to find out.

When I showed up at her house, I expected to have to wait, to go get her, to carry various pieces of luggage. To my pleasant surprise, she and her dad were waiting outside. He tossed her case in my car, said hello to me, hugged Bellamy goodbye, and disappeared.

Bellamy poked her head in the window and grinned, her eyes scanning me up and down. "Hello, Hot Huntley."

As nicknames went, I didn't hate it.

CHAPTER 2

Bellamy opened the door, plopped inside, and buckled her belt. Right away my car felt different, more hers, less mine. She was that type, a girl who spilled into and took over all available spaces. Her hair did it now. Her curls were wild and springy, unable to be pent up by the band attempting to hold them together. She wasn't my type, but she was cute in an uncontained and bohemian way. I liked tall girls, thin girls, girls who always looked neat and well put together. Bellamy was short, curvy, and always wore t-shirts covered by her brother's flannels, like she was about to audition for the role of lumberjack mascot or something.

"Bellamy, you're looking well," I said, and it wasn't a lie. There were no surprises with Bellamy, and I liked that about her. I hadn't seen her in months, and she looked exactly the same. Meanwhile I had grown a few inches, filled out, and matured.

She laughed as if I'd told a joke. I glanced at her, puzzled, and she laughed again. "You're funny."

"Okay," I drawled. "Ready?"

In answer, she gave me a little salute. I faced forward. *Weird.*

"So, what's up, Huntley? How many girlfriends you have now?"

"None," I said.

"What? That's not possible."

"Why is that not possible?"

"Because have you seen you? You're all pretty now. And you have the nice boy chivalrous manners. You're the total package. And now you're blushing. So cute." She poked my bicep. I shrugged it away.

"What about you? Any boyfriends?"

"Yeah, right. It was a tight contest between Jedadiah and Harrison for a while," she said, naming two guys from our homeschool circle who were so lacking in social skills they gave all homeschoolers a bad name.

I laughed and she continued, "I really thought you would have picked up some public school fresh meat this year. I mean, wasn't that kind of the point of going?"

"Nah. I had friends, but no one like that. Mostly I wanted the immersive high school experience with no distractions."

"The immersive high school experience. That's hot," she said.

I gave her bicep a shove without taking my eyes off the road. "Shutty."

"My time is now," she added.

"What does that mean?"

"It means I'm going to get me a weather camp boyfriend."

I grimaced. "What?"

"It's camp. It's like the law that people pair up." She regarded me with a serious expression. "It could be you."

I darted her a glance. "What are you talking about?"

"We could have a camp thing. Then when we get home we go our separate ways and it will be our secret." She wagged her brows at me.

"Uh, no," I said.

"Why not?"

"Because I don't see you like that."

"Why not?"

"Because we've known each other forever, since we were born."

"So longevity is a point against me? Can you only date people you just met? Seems risky."

"It's not longevity. It's…" I trailed off. Nothing in my experience had prepared me for this conversation.

"Are you saying I'm fat?"

"What?" My head whipped to look at her. She was curvy, for certain, but not fat. "No. Of course not. I would never."

"Ugly?" she tried.

"No, you're not ugly. You're…you're fine."

"I'm *fine*?"

I swiped a hand over my face. When did this conversation get away from me? "Not that kind of fine. You're okay."

"Oh, so it's my personality you can't stand," she said.

"What? That's not…How did we get here?"

"You were telling me all the reasons I repulse you," she said.

"You don't repulse me," I contradicted.

"Really? So you're saying you're attracted to me?"

"What? No, I'm not…Why does it have to be one or the other? There's plenty of room in the middle here. I am neither repulsed by nor attracted to you. You're just Bellamy, girl I've known forever, the end."

"I think you're missing a real opportunity here, Huntley. I mean, I'm offering you two weeks of unsolicited makeout time with a no strings agreement on the other end of it. Have you thought this through?"

I gave her shoulder a shove without taking my eyes off the road. "Stop it. No means no."

"Wow, okay. But as your lifelong friend with whom you apparently share zero attraction, let me offer you this advice. You'd better be careful. I was serious about the pairings. Girls are going to be gunning for you. Choose wisely."

"Okay, Bellamy," I said.

"You've been warned," she said, pointing at me. "What's new with Haven?"

"Nothing."

"She still with the guy?"

"Yeah, I think they're lifers," I said.

"How is that possible? I mean, seriously. We're babies. How can you meet the man you want to spend the rest of your life with already? There are so many people out there. Think what she could be missing out on."

"She and Sutton really love each other. I don't think either one of them believe they're missing out on anything. They're sweet together, kind and supporting. What more could you want?"

"Passion, baby," Bellamy said. "Do you think Haven has that?"

I grimaced. "Ew, that's my sister you're talking about. I never want the answer to that question."

"Why not? Everyone deserves passion, even you, Hot Huntley Mulligan."

"What do you mean even me? Why not me?" I was seriously beginning to remember why I didn't like her. It was because of conversations like this that went in circles and made my head hurt. Half the time I had no idea what she was talking about.

"You're not, you know, the passionate sort."

"Yes, I am," I said.

"I can't picture it," she said.

"I'm passionate about all kinds of things. The weather, bees, my family and friends, God."

She snorted a laugh and slapped her hand over her mouth. "Did you include bees in that sentence? Are you going to use that on a dating profile? 'Yo, girl, come check out my apiary. You like honey? 'Cause you're naturally sweet.'"

"Shut up." I don't think I had ever told a person outside my younger siblings to shut up before, but I meant it. She was getting on my nerves.

"Come over to my skep. We'll do the mating dance," she continued undaunted, clutching her stomach and giggling at her own jokes.

I shook my head, trying and failing to block out her voice.

"I feel the *sting* of attraction for you." She poked me. "Might as well laugh. I've got a million of them."

"You're mental," I said, and meant it. Predictably, Bellamy laughed.

"I'm going to keep an eye out for a girl who likes to wear black and yellow. Clearly seasonal allergies are a deal breaker. I mean, how would she handle pollination?"

"You need medication," I said, but I was smiling a little.

"I need a man, and since you're not up to the task yourself, you're going to have to be my wingman."

"What does that mean?"

"Like you scout potential guys for me, put in a good word, that sort of thing. And obviously I'll be your wing girl while you look for potential queens." She elbowed me. "That was another bee joke."

"The best jokes are the ones that require an explanation," I said.

"No, the best jokes are the ones people laugh at. It doesn't do you much good to be hot now if you're lacking a sense of humor."

"I am not lacking a sense of humor. I have an amazing sense of humor. I just don't usually like to find humor at the expense of other people."

"'For what do we live, but to make sport for our neighbors, and laugh at them in our turn?'"

"Why is that familiar?" I asked.

"Jane Austen, baby, the GOAT romance author."

"I think that might be the first time in history anyone has ever referred to Jane Austen as a GOAT."

"She's also the OG, the Original Gangster of love."

"Wow." I tapped the car's GPS. "How far have we got to go here?"

"You should cherish this time with me. This might be the last time we ever see each other."

"Are you planning to die soon?" I asked.

"Don't sound so hopeful. You're graduated now, and I only have a year left. Soon our paths will diverge, and who knows if they'll ever cross again? Although maybe that should be some kind of test for us, like that movie."

"I'm sort of breaking a rule by even asking, but what movie?"

"*Serendipity*. These two people met and fell in love, but then separated and left things up to fate. Maybe that's what's going to happen with us, like fifteen years from now we'll run into each other at the market and you'll say, 'Remember when we rode together to weather camp and you made all those delightful jokes about bees? I think that was when I began to fall in love with you.' And I'll say, 'If only you had taken me up on my offer in the car to be your camp girlfriend. But alas I met my husband, the Surgeon General, at that camp, and now we're having our fifth baby. You can't tell by looking at me, of course, because I've miraculously maintained my figure, despite my love of chocolate cheesecake.'" She shook her head. "Sad."

"Mental," I repeated, shaking my head.

"So what kind of girl do you like, Hunt? How come no one calls you Hunt?"

"Because it's not my name. Do people call you Bell?"

"I wish. I've always wanted a cutesy nickname. That could be our thing, Hunt and Bell."

"We don't have a thing. Don't call me Hunt. I will never call you Bell."

"Belle means beauty," she said.

"It also means that shrill, annoying thing that makes a high-pitched noise incessantly," I said.

She gasped. "Did the Sainted Huntley Mulligan just insult me?"

"I've been doing it this entire trip. You're choosing not to hear or believe it," I said.

"You know you love me. You have to; it's the law when you've known someone as long as we've known each other. Plus, we're kind of classmates, you know? And our school is way too small to have enemies." She pointed between us. "Speaking of school, where are you going next year?"

"I'm taking a gap year to think about my options," I said.

"Options? What options? Your future in the NBA? Peace Corps? What?"

"My major, meteorology or medicine," I said.

"You either want to study the clouds or save lives. They're so much alike, I can see why you're confused. What will be your deciding factor, do you think?"

"This camp, maybe," I said.

"Hmm." She faced forward, staring thoughtfully through the front windshield.

"No snappy comebacks?"

"No because now I realize that I'm only a year away from needing to make my own life-altering decisions. Suddenly it all became real. I can always count on you to be a downer." She patted my leg and left her hand lying there when she finished. I glanced at it and then at her.

"Bellamy."

"Hmm," she said, still facing forward.

"What are you doing?"

"Testing to see what would happen if I sneaked up on you. Like, offered some innocuously intimate touch, if you would realize you are, in fact, attracted to me, pull the car over, and we'd make out."

I picked her hand up by the wrist and plopped it in her own lap. "No."

"Someday I have the feeling you're going to regret this entire car ride," she said.

"Someday starts right now," I mumbled. She got very quiet. I thought maybe I had actually hurt her feelings, but when I glanced at her to check, I saw her shoulders shaking with laughter.

CHAPTER 3

I thought I would feel relieved to arrive at camp and have done with Bellamy. But when we pulled onto the sprawling college campus that would be our home for the next ten days, I felt a pressing anxiety in my chest. Haven was right, this was my first time away from home. Ever. Suddenly Bellamy felt comfortingly familiar.

"What are you doing?" she asked as we stepped from the car and I shouldered all of her bags.

"Carrying your stuff," I said.

"That's sweet, but there's not much. I can get it," she assured me.

"You think my parents would allow that? Come on." I hunched her bag higher on my shoulder and led the way to her dorm. Her room was on the second floor.

"Want me to carry some of that? I kind of packed a lot, I wasn't sure what to bring, you know?"

"It's fine, I've got it." I wasn't, I was sort of breathless, but no way was I going to tell her that. I stood aside while she checked in and got her key. She opened her door and we stepped inside the room.

"This is so surreal. It feels like we're actually going to college, you know?"

"I know," I said because it was the same way I felt, like this was somehow a bigger deal than it was. It was two weeks of camp and I'd be going back home. But next year I might be going away for real, and so would Bellamy. We stared around the empty little dorm room. "Wonder who your roommate will be."

"You mean you wonder if she'll be hot," she said.

"No, I meant I wonder if she'll be crazy or scary. She could stab you in your sleep."

"Comforting, Huntley, thank you."

I stared around her room again. Clearly, it was time for me to go. "Want to come with me to my room?"

Bellamy tossed me a smile. "Sure." She tucked her key into her pocket and followed me back to the car where I unloaded my suitcase.

"Did Haven pack for you?" she guessed.

"I'm an actual adult now," I said.

"I'll take that as a yes," she said.

"Shut up. She's really good at it and I really hate it. Plus it gave her time to stuff things in my pack, secret treasures."

"You guys are the cutest," she said.

"We really are," I agreed. Some people didn't like their siblings. I couldn't imagine. Haven had always been my best friend.

Now it was Bellamy's turn to follow me up to my room. My roommate had already checked in and unloaded, taking the bottom bunk. I set my stuff in my room and Bellamy helped me make my bed. Belatedly I wondered if that was something I should have helped her do, but it seemed more like a girly thing than a guy thing to offer. My sisters were all like that, always making things comfortable and pretty. My brothers and I didn't put as much thought into the details as they did.

"Thanks," I said when my bed was fully made. I gave it a pat. "What do we do now?"

She glanced around, as if for inspiration. "Mingle, I guess?"

I nodded, but neither of us made a move to leave. After glancing around the room again, we made eye contact and laughed. "We're not representing homeschoolers well right now. We can go out there and meet people. They're just other kids, like us."

"Yes," I agreed. "Let's go." I tugged the sleeve of her flannel and led the way this time, a strange thing for me to do. I was used to following Haven's lead. We walked to the quad but it seemed empty. It was such a large campus and we were a small group. Seemingly everyone had gotten the memo to be somewhere else. I knew we should go and find them, but I didn't want to. Bellamy seemed content to hang back, too, her earlier bravado gone.

"Maybe we could wander campus awhile. It's really pretty," Bellamy observed.

"Sure," I agreed. We began to walk, checking out the place as if we belonged, as if we knew what we were doing and where we were going. As if we weren't a couple of kids away from home for the first time.

"When'd you get so tall, Huntley?" Bellamy asked, shading her eyes as she squinted up at me.

"It was a gradual process," I said.

"I still think of you as being my size. Then I catch a glimpse of you and realize you're not." She shook her head as if to clear it. "It's disorienting."

"Sorry?" I said.

"You should be," she said, punching me lightly in the shoulder. I reached out and squeezed the back of her neck and then thought maybe I shouldn't have. My family was affectionate. I was learning not everyone else was. But Bellamy didn't seem to think anything of the touch. Her cheeks weren't pink, and she didn't seem uncomfortable or embarrassed. All of a sudden I realized I was going to have to go two weeks without a hug from my mom, Haven, my little sisters, without a hug from anybody.

"What's wrong?" Bellamy asked when I stopped short and stared into space.

I faced her, my mouth going dry with dread and panic. What was I doing here? I didn't want to leave home, didn't want to grow up, go away, leave my family. Independence was for other people, not me. I licked my lips. "Maybe…maybe we should be together."

"What?"

"Maybe you should be my fake girlfriend," I blurted.

She blinked at me and tipped her head, studying me. "First, I never said fake. I said *camp*."

"Is there a difference?" I asked.

"Yes, the difference being one is fake and one is real but temporary. Second, the offer was only good in the car. Now that we're here…" she spread her hands and looked around.

I rolled my eyes, summoning my earlier annoyance. "Come on, Bellamy."

"Come on what, Huntley? Because I know what this is about, and it's not very flattering," she said.

"What is this about?"

"This is about the fact that you hate change and got scared and want me to be your comfort item from home," she said.

My insides squirmed with how close she was to the truth. " I am not scared. If two guys burst from the woods right now and tried to mug you, I would jump to your defense. I would give my life to protect you. I am not afraid."

"What if two girls jumped from the forest and said they wanted to play Seven Minutes in Heaven with you, what would you do then?"

"Probably text Sutton to see what that is," I said. I let out a breath. "I just think we're out of our element here. It would be nice to have someone, like an alliance."

Bellamy crossed her arms over her chest and studied the horizon. "Are you even attracted to me?"

I should probably blurt a ready, "Absolutely," but I couldn't. Instead I studied her for a few beats. She was short and curvy and cute, adorable really, with her crazy curly hair and big brown eyes. She wasn't my type, but I could objectively say she wasn't bad to look at. "You're cute," I said at last.

It must have been the wrong thing to say because she huffed a sigh and squinted up at me again. "Sea otters are cute. Guinea pigs are cute. Am I kissable?"

I couldn't stop my grimace. The thought of kissing Bellamy was… ew. "I've known you so long. It's hard to see you that way."

"That's fair," she agreed. "How about this. We'll give it two days, two days in which we scope out the competition, see what this place has to offer. Maybe you'll meet the girl of your dreams, maybe I'll meet the guy of my dreams. If in two days that doesn't happen, we'll reassess and see if we want to continue on this path. If we don't, no hard feelings. If we do then…" she floundered. "I don't actually know what happens then. Deal?" She held out her hand for me to shake.

I stared at it. "What do we do in the meantime? Are we supposed to ignore each other until then while we're making our assessments?"

"Of course not. We'll stay platonic, like we've always been. You'll just have to control your raging hormonal urges when it comes to me," she said.

She still held out her hand. I took it and kissed the back of it. "I'll try."

Her lashes fluttered a little, as if the unexpected gesture took her by surprise. I didn't hate that look. In fact, I kind of liked it.

CHAPTER 4

We found people. They were mingling in the lobby of the cafeteria, eating and drinking. We looked like a group of adults, talking and laughing, except all of our drinks were alcohol-free and the food consisted of cheese doodles and Doritos.

Even though I'd known Bellamy for years and years, I realized I had only ever seen her in social situations where we already knew everyone. At homeschool gatherings she was always at the center, outgoing and talkative. I was usually the one who hung in the background, overwhelmed by all the noise and chatter. But here things were already different. We stepped into the room and Bellamy shrank back slightly, probably not enough that other people who didn't know her would realize. But for me, who was used to her, it was unusual and curious behavior. Worse, it compelled me to be the front man for once. I tugged her sleeve and led her forward, approaching a group of other kids already immersed in conversation and laughter that came to a pause.

"Hey," I said, giving the group a friendly smile. "I'm Huntley. This is Bellamy."

"Hi," Bellamy said, still sounding uncharacteristically shy. The shyness made me feel something I had never felt toward her before —protective.

"I'm Curt," the guy said. His eyes slid over me and landed on Bellamy. Apparently he liked what he saw because his smile widened.

"I'm Hillary," the girl added. She was tall and blond, her hair neatly smoothed behind a wide headband. Bellamy caught my eye and we shared a smile because it seemed we'd met our matches. "Did you guys come together?"

"We're old friends," Bellamy said. "How about you guys?"

"We didn't come together, but we've known each other a while because we're in the same robotics league," Curt said.

"Robotics?" Bellamy perked up. "Have you made yourself a butler and or dog?"

"No," Curt drawled, "mostly simple machines, though I've been working on a battle bot."

"If that battle bot can't fetch toys or the mail, you're wasting your life," Bellamy said.

Curt looked at her the way I usually looked at her, as if he wasn't sure what to make of her. But there was something more there, too— amusement and attraction. "What's with the flannels, Curt Cobain?"

"Is that your namesake?" Bellamy asked.

"No, are you dodging the question? It's the middle of summer," he replied, tapping her foot with his.

"Okay, wow, apparently someone's gotten a jump start on the weather curriculum. I'm already intimidated by your genius," Bellamy replied.

"One eighty," he said, tapping his temple.

"That's coincidentally also the degrees it would take for me to walk away and forget this conversation," Bellamy replied.

Curt laughed. "I see you don't have a drink, Mr. Cobain."

"Nothing gets by you, Ace."

"Would you care to accompany me to the snack table?"

"This is so sudden. Yes," Bellamy said and, just like that, they set off together, talking and laughing, leaving me alone with Hillary.

"Well, that was fast," Hillary said.

"Bellamy's always been advanced," I said. "Where are you from?"

"I'm from here, about a half hour away."

"Did you graduate this year?"

"Yes, this is my last stop before college."

"And where is college?"

"Dartmouth."

"Wow," I said, duly impressed.

"What about you?"

"I graduated, but I'm taking a gap year."

"Huh," she said. I wracked my brain for something else to say but came up blank. Why was this so hard? I was usually good at meeting new people, was well known for being friendly. Hillary gazed across the room where Bellamy and Curt now stood at the center of a new group of people, talking and laughing. That was more like the Bellamy I knew. I was glad she was finding her footing. If only I could say the same.

"Want to go see what they're up to?" I suggested.

"Sure," she said, sounding relieved. We trooped over to what had clearly become the center of fun in the room. Bellamy stood at the helm, shaking her head while people around her called out guesses.

"What's going on?" Hillary asked.

"We're trying to guess why Bellamy's wearing a flannel. If we get it right, she'll take it off," a guy said, adding, "your grandpa died and that was his favorite shirt."

"No, and creepy, *ew*," Bellamy said.

"Leukemia."

"Abusive boyfriend."

"Abusive parents."

"No, what is wrong with you people? So dark," Bellamy said, shaking her head.

"I know why," I announced. Everyone stopped to look at me, including Bellamy who squinted up at me appraisingly.

"You know nothing," she said, trying to read my poker face.

Thanks to actual poker with Haven, who used any weakness to her competitive advantage, my poker face was stellar. "I know everything," I said, and it was mostly true. Bellamy used to be a tomboy until one summer a few years ago when everything changed. That was when she had started wearing the flannels.

"Tell us," one of the guys urged.

Bellamy and I squared off, staring. Her expression was full of wariness but also challenge. She knew I knew, but she also knew I wouldn't be comfortable blurting the truth to a group of strangers. I crossed the divide between us and leaned close to whisper in her ear. "It's because one summer you suddenly realized you're a girl, and you've never been comfortable enough to own it."

She looked up at me, cheeks flushing pleasantly, one hand perched on my chest—to push me away or pull me close? And then she dropped her hand, slid out of the flannel, and tied it around her waist.

"Kind of hating you at this moment," she whispered.

"Really? I'm kind of feeling the opposite," I said, and then one of our instructors arrived and called everyone to order.

CHAPTER 5

*H*ow's camp?

Haven waited until bedtime to text. Or at least my bedtime. Everyone else in the dorm showed little sign of turning out their lights or limiting their noise. I debated where to start or what to tell her. That, as I suspected, I didn't fit? That everyone seemed more worldly and wise than I was? That I felt like the country mouse on holiday? That I missed her? That I missed home? That my roommate, Jeremy, while nice, was a major partier and possible womanizer?

Thinking of fake dating Bellamy, was what I finally decided to impart. I sat back and watched the reply bubbles appear and disappear three times before she finally responded.

Her idea, I take it?

Was there any doubt?

Are you going to do it?

Was I? I still didn't know, and I had a whole other day to figure it out. Tonight had been...illuminating, to say the least. After Bellamy took off her flannel, she had even more male attention because, well, there's no polite way to say it without sounding like a pig. She's stacked. I try not to notice that stuff about girls. Honestly. I mean, I have sisters, so it's not like I'm not aware how the other half lives nor all the stuff they have to put up with from guys. And I would never want someone ogling them the way the guys here were ogling Bellamy. But also, I couldn't seem to stop ogling Bellamy.

Still, that wasn't enough reason to go out with her. Was it? Not that it was completely up to me. She and Curt seemed to be hitting it off nicely, as evidenced by the fact that, at the end of the meeting, he walked her back to her dorm. Hillary and I followed in their wake, trying and failing to make conversation. She was pretty, but things couldn't seem to get off the ground with her. I suspected she liked Curt, if the resentful way she darted looks at Bellamy was any indication.

What do you think I should do? I wasn't averse to having Haven order my life, even from a distance.

Sorry, little brother. You're on your own.

Two minutes, I reminded her. That was how much seniority she had on me in life, but they had always mattered. In a lot of ways, I did act like the little brother while she remained the unchallenged leader. It was only when it came to protecting her that we switched roles, and not by her choice. But she was a foot smaller than me. How could I not always feel the need to take care of her?

Sutton wants to know if she's hot. I am not equipped to answer that question.

My fingers hovered over my phone as I thought of Bellamy. Before today, I knew how I would answer. And now? *Tell him yes.*

I was about to change out and get ready for bed when a knock sounded on my door. Bellamy, Curt, and Hillary stood on the other side.

"Party in Cullen's room. You in?" Curt asked.

I already knew there was a party in Cullen's room. It was where my roommate was. I opened my mouth to tell them no but caught sight of Bellamy's expression, clearly pleading.

"Sure," I said slowly.

"Great, I'm going to help him get ready. Be there in a minute," Bellamy said. She ducked inside uninvited and closed the door behind her, leaning on it. *"Thank you,"* she mouthed.

"What's up?" I whispered.

She stood on her toes to check the peephole, making sure the others were gone before she answered. "I changed my mind."

"You don't want to go to the party?"

"No, I want to go to the party. I meant I changed my mind about us."

I sat in the uncomfortable plastic chair beside the desk. Bellamy began to wander around the room, arms crossed over her chest. She was once again wearing the flannel, I noted with a combination of relief and disappointment.

"You want to be with Curt," I guessed.

"No, I want to be with you." She whirled, facing me, arms still crossed over her chest.

"You…what? I thought you liked Curt."

"I do. He's cute and funny and smart, kind of a hot geek."

"Then why do you want to be with me?"

"I want to do the thing you said. I want to fake date."

"Why?"

She turned away from me and picked up something from Jeremy's desk. I was by no means an expert, but I thought maybe it was a bong. Bellamy turned it over, examining it. "Have you ever wanted something and then when it happened you realized you weren't ready for it?"

"Yes."

"It's like that."

I studied her, shoulders tensed and hunched, one arm pressed tightly to her waist. "Did he do something to you?"

She shook her head.

"Did he?" I pressed, more insistent now. Maybe I went overboard on the protectiveness thing, but from what I saw girls needed someone strong and capable on their side once in a while.

"No, but he was looking at me like…like he wanted things to happen between us that I'm not ready for. It freaked me out, and you're the only way I know how to backpedal. You're my escape pod." She whirled to face me with a smile. "Do you mind?"

Did I? I hadn't thought about scoring a camp girlfriend until she brought it up. The more I thought of it, the more the idea appealed to me. But Hillary was the only person I had so far been attracted to, and the chemistry seemed to be lacking. "What would it entail?"

"Forming an alliance."

"What does that mean to you?" I asked.

"Looking out for each other, sticking together, having each other's backs."

"I thought we already did that by virtue of being lifelong friends," I said.

"It would be maybe a little bit more. We'd have to…" she paused and pushed the hair off her face. She was that type of girl, the one who always had hair falling out of its clip, obscuring her eyes, sticking to her lips, brushing her cheeks. Suddenly I realized a low level anxiety about her hair. I wanted to bundle it up and push it away from her face for keeps. "We'd have to sell it," she finished in a rush, pushing at her hair again.

"How exactly would we do that?"

"We'd have to look like we're a couple."

"How would that be different than being a couple?" I asked.

"Minus all the feels."

"What kind of feels?" I asked.

"Huntley Mulligan," she exclaimed, plopping her hands on her hips.

"I meant am I allowed to touch you? I'm an affectionate person. I don't want to have to edit myself around you, and I don't want you to misconstrue every touch as something else."

"We can hold hands and hug, but I think we should draw the line at kissing. Too real."

"Too true," I agreed.

"There's going to be a tricky conversion period because I've been hanging out with Curt all day. I'm going to have to faze him out and faze you in," she said, worrying her lip between her teeth.

"I've never been in a love triangle before," I said, leaning forward and resting my elbows on my knees.

"I've been in tons," Bellamy said. I couldn't tell if she was joking. She took a deep breath. "We should probably go."

"Why are we going to this party?"

"Because it's a party," she said.

"Have you ever been to a party?" I asked.

"I've been to parties with you."

I almost laughed. She sounded like me a year ago, before high school. "This party won't be like that one. It's not going to be like anything you're used to."

"How do you know?"

"Because I know."

"But how?" she pressed.

"Because at school this year, the people I'm friends with, they party. A lot. In fact Sutton's kind of an alcoholic. He had to stop partying after he got drunk and texted Haven in the middle of the night. My dad went to go get him. And then his dad drove drunk and crashed into a tree. It's a whole big thing. Suffice it to say this party will not be fun for us."

"I still want to see, to know what it's like. Isn't that the point of this camp? To experience new things?"

"I suppose," I said. "It's just really late."

"It's eleven. You're eighteen, Grandpa. Live a little."

"We've been fake dating five minutes and you're already for real nagging me," I said.

She smiled. "Would you prefer I fake nag you?" she offered.

"How about no nagging?"

"It's not in my nature to not give you a hard time, Hot Huntley."

"Do you actually think I'm hot?" I blurted.

"Your hotness is not up for debate. You're indisputably hot. You've got the body and the face and someone apparently taught you how to dress." She waved distractedly in my direction.

"But are you attracted to me?" I demanded.

"Are you attracted to me?" she countered.

"I…don't know," I said slowly.

She shrugged. "We don't have to be attracted to each other. We just have to pretend to be."

"Remind me why again?"

She came over and sat in front of me cross-legged on the floor. "I guess, Huntley, there's nothing in it for you. I guess I'm asking you to do it for me, as a friend. Because…because I'm scared and I trust you and I could really use you on my team right now."

I had known her for seventeen years, and I had never heard her so earnest before. I reached out to touch her cheek. She leaned closer, pressing it into my palm. "Are you sure nothing happened to you?"

"Curt didn't do anything to me," she assured me. It wasn't until later that I would understand the distinction in her statement.

CHAPTER 6

"So this is a party," Bellamy said.

It was likely tame, compared to some. Parker, Sutton, Reagan, and Addison had told me some of what went on at the parties I hadn't attended, and it seemed much worse than what I was seeing. There were a few bottles of some kind of liquor, likely something somebody had sneaked from home. Not everyone was drinking. Those who were passed the bottle, sharing it with no cups and no regard to germs. Even if I had been tempted to drink, which I wasn't, I couldn't stomach the thought of sharing a bottle with so many strangers. Neither could Bellamy if the grimace she gave the bottle was any indication.

"So many people going to have cold sores after this night," she whispered.

"If the bottle doesn't get them, then the kissing will," I said, nodding to a corner where a few couples were already paired off and making out. Again, not everyone was locking lips, but enough so that it was obvious this wasn't our kind of party.

"No musical chairs?" she whispered, and I laughed. That was actu-ally something one of our parents would try to foist on us at a homeschool gathering. In their defense, they had to cater to all ages and we both had a few younger siblings.

Curt had apparently been keeping an eye out for Bellamy because he made a beeline to us, Hillary reluctantly in his wake. "You made it. I was starting to worry."

"Huntley couldn't decide between this black polo shirt or the charcoal one," Bellamy said, tugging on my sleeve as she smiled up at me. I did have a broad assortment of similarly colored shirts.

"Decision fatigue is not a victimless crime," I said. "By keeping my clothing choices simple, I follow in the footsteps of the greats."

"Lucky for you they all look good," she replied. Curt faltered, looking between us. I faltered, too, not sure how exactly to help her faze myself in while fazing him out.

"Whose room is this again?" I asked.

"Cullen," Hillary said, pointing to a guy who was tipping back one of the bottles of what I now read as vodka, taking a big swig. "If you guys want a drink, you'd better get there soon. They're disappearing quickly."

"I'm good," I said, not even trying to hide my grimace as some of the liquid seeped out of the bottle and ran down Cullen's face.

"Mmm, shared bacteria," Bellamy said, rubbing her stomach.

Curt laughed. "Want to dance?" He tugged her hand.

"Definitely," she said, grabbing my hand and Hillary's so the four of us trooped onto the makeshift dance floor together. It was a fast song, so it wasn't odd that we were moving en masse. Curt's hand rested possessively on Bellamy's waist a few times, attempting to draw her away. I reached out, clasped her hand, and tugged her to me.

"Be right back," I said. I had to say it loudly to be heard over the music. She trotted behind me as I led her to the far side of the room. Someone had attached their phone to some speakers and it was now loudly blaring techno music, so loud that we had to cover our ears as we approached. I brought up a song on my phone and swapped it for the one on the speakers. No one seemed to notice, or if they did, they didn't comment as swing music began to play.

"Oh," Bellamy breathed, a little startle of delight that made me smile. "I forgot about this."

She was one of the few people who knew I could dance. I was glad she had forgotten. It gave me hope other people would, too. Though now that I was about to put myself on display in a big way, I wasn't helping my cause.

Dancing is an oddly misogynistic activity because it doesn't matter so much what the girl does or how good she is. It matters more how well the guy can lead. And I was an excellent lead. Bellamy was pliable and enthusiastic, allowing me to spin her and swing her around the dance floor. A few other people joined in, making us less conspicuous. After a couple of songs, I went to retrieve my phone, once again bringing Bellamy with me.

"That was, wow," Hillary said when we returned. *Now* she was looking at me with interest. What was it with girls and dancing? "You guys do that often?"

"That was the first time, actually," I said. Curt was looking at Bellamy much the same as Hillary was now looking at me. For that reason, I kept hold of her hand.

"He usually dances with Haven," Bellamy said.

I rolled my eyes at her. *Thanks for that.*

"Who's Haven?" Hillary asked.

"Mutual friend," Bellamy said, giving my hand a squeeze.

"You want to take off?" Curt asked Bellamy. What was it with this guy? Subtlety was apparently lost on him.

"Yeah, I think we should," I said, eyeing Bellamy. "I need to talk to you about something. Catch you guys tomorrow." I led Bellamy behind me, not waiting for a reply.

"Wow, Huntley, wow," she said when we were safely in the hallway.

"Too much?" I asked, but I was smiling.

"Uh, no. That was freaking amazing. It's like you've been programed to be on perfect fake boyfriend mode. I mean, seriously. And the dancing put it over the top. I don't know, I might have to keep you when this is over."

"Absolutely. If all goes well, we could spin this fake relationship into a fake marriage."

We walked in silence across the quad, still hand in hand.

"Why did you get all quiet? I didn't actually freak you out about keeping you, did I? Because I was totally kidding," she said.

"No, I know. It was what I said. I had one of those moments where I realized I probably am only a few years away from getting married and it freaked me out. This past year stuff like that keeps happening, like suddenly the veil is lifted and real life slips in for a minute. Like with Haven going away to school soon. It's getting harder and harder to pretend things are going to stay the same forever."

"Oh," she said softly. We walked in silence a while longer until we reached her dorm. "It is kind of weird, when you think about it. Like, how does it actually happen? How do you know when you've met the one person you want to spend forever with? How can anyone possibly know that? How can anyone possibly be ready for that?" We faced each other.

"I have no idea," I said.

"Is it some big sign from heaven, like *this is the one* flashes over someone's head?"

I shrugged.

That must not have been a good enough answer because she kept asking. "I don't understand how you could ever know when you're ready. What was it like for Haven?"

"I'm pretty sure it was unavoidable for them. They couldn't stay away from each other, no matter how hard they tried."

"I can't imagine how that works. Like, how do you pick one person and be like, you, you're the person I want to wake up to for the rest of my life." She shuddered.

"If I think about it too much, I spiral toward an anxiety attack. Actually, if I think about anything too much, I spiral toward anxiety. It's why I have so many hobbies, to keep my mind from imploding."

She blew out a breath. "That escalated quickly." The air around us felt oppressive now. My chest was tight with the weight of too many serious things bearing down on me: Haven leaving, my unknown career choice, the far-off future with a wife and kids and bills. Bellamy rested her palms on my chest and smoothed them in little circles, like she was buffing a car. "Maybe the key is to focus on each moment, without allowing ourselves to think of the future."

"That's not what our parents say. They're always telling us to think about our futures." My parents were full of directives about what my future should look like. *What kind of man do you want to be?* My father was famous for asking the question to me and me brothers. *The choices you make today will determine who you will become.* The pressure of that was immense, too much. I felt like one little misstep would trigger a cataclysmic chain of events that had the power to destroy the rest of my life.

"But we're at camp now. We've entered a magical wormhole where there is no future, there's only now. So let's agree right now to stop worrying about what happens after, to not think about Haven leaving or pending college and career choices. For the next few weeks we will live in the moment. We will have fun and not worry or think about anything. If it feels good, do it. That's going to be our brand new philosophy until this is over."

By "this" I didn't know if she meant camp or our temporary fake relationship. "If that were true, I would kiss you right now." I had no idea where that came from, but it seemed like the right thing to say in the moment. And if I'm being honest, I did want to kiss her right then.

She shook her head at me, but she was smiling.

"What?" I prompted.

"You've got game, Huntley Mulligan. But you know what?"

"What?"

"So do I." She grasped my shirt, stood on her toes, and brushed her lips softly to mine. And then, before I could reach for her or think to continue, she let me go and backed toward her dorm. "I'll see you tomorrow."

"See you," I said. She disappeared inside but I remained standing on the sidewalk, staring at her building and trying to put the pieces of the day together. This morning Bellamy hadn't been on my mind. Nothing had been on my mind, except getting to weather camp. And now, for possibly the first time ever, the atmosphere had taken a back seat to my current circumstances. Because now the thing I most looked forward to tomorrow wasn't the first day of camp, it was the first day of my fake relationship with Bellamy.

CHAPTER 7

In the morning, my head felt clearer. The problem with having a flirtation with a girl I'd known forever was that she was a girl I'd known forever. Our families were good friends. It was part of the reason I had known her so long and had seen her so often. If you asked my mom, she would likely say Bellamy's mom was her best friend. Could I really risk our cozy, familial relationship for a camp fling, fake or not?

I would tell her we were better off as friends, that the road we were on was a bad idea. Of course I could only tell her that if she showed up to class. She had already missed breakfast. Now class was getting ready to start, and it looked like she might miss that, too. Was I supposed to go get her? Was it a fake camp boyfriend thing to do to pick her up from her dorm in the morning? Was that why she hadn't come, because I had already failed in our pretend relationship? In either case, her lateness annoyed me, as it always did. Could I be with a girl who was perpetually tardy, even in an imaginary realm?

Just as class was about to begin, Bellamy skidded into the chair next to me. I turned to her with annoyance that quickly fled. Today she wore a short sleeved button up shirt with tiny pink flowers all over it. Her hair was down and much longer than I remembered. Her cheeks were flushed, probably from sprinting to make it on time. Her lips looked bigger and softer than I remembered. All of a sudden I remembered the feathery brush of them last night. When had Bellamy gotten so pretty? So soft and pink and feminine? It was like sharing space with a rosebud.

"What?" she whispered as I continued to stare at her, ignoring everything our instructor was now saying.

I leaned closer to whisper. "You missed breakfast."

She tipped her head so her breath now tickled my ear when she answered. "I hate breakfast."

The instructor cleared his throat, giving us a pointed glance. I eased my notebook closer and wrote her a note. *It's the most important meal of the day.*

The ad council was made for people like you, she replied.

You shouldn't skip breakfast, I returned.

Do you get a cut of the breakfast profits? she asked.

My hand hovered over the paper before I wrote, *Maybe I missed you.*

Her hand hovered the same length of time before she replied, *Maybe I'll show up sometime. For you.*

The class was immersive and intense, the kind that required a lot of mathematical calculations. We would be making predictions about the weather the old fashioned way, without the benefit of a computer. This was what I was here for, to focus on the work, to try and figure out how much of a role it played in my future. And yet I couldn't stop my eyes and thoughts from straying to Bellamy. How had I never realized how good she smelled? How intently she focused on her work? A furrow worked its way between her brows and I leaned closer.

"What's the problem?" I asked and she jumped a little as if she'd forgotten I was there.

"Stuck on this calculation," she said.

I pulled her notebook closer and studied her math. "Here," I said, tapping the paper with my eraser. "This should be a three, not a four." When I glanced up, she was looking at me, likely in the same way I had been looking at her all morning, as if seeing me anew. And maybe liking what she saw.

"Thank you," she whispered.

"You're welcome," I replied. I faced forward again, feeling vaguely disoriented. We had done homework together countless times. When we were younger, our moms used to combine school days once a week so that we were all piled in a room together, like a real school. Bellamy, Haven, and I had always been lumped together. But it had never been like that, so intense and breathless.

We broke for lunch. I stood and stretched. Bellamy did the same. We eyed each other, a little hesitant, a little wary. We had placed ourselves in a new normal that neither of us knew how to deal with. I both wanted to undo it and go back and keep pressing into the unknown. It was exhilarating and terrifying all at once. What if Bellamy and I were together and actually ended up having fun? What if Bellamy and I were together and ended up being awful?

"Maybe we should have a conversation," she said.

"I think yes," I agreed. We turned to go and ran, almost literally, into Curt and Hillary.

"What's up?" Curt said, addressing Bellamy and not me.

"Just grabbing lunch," Bellamy replied.

"Us too. Let's sit together," he said as he positioned himself beside her. Somehow I ended up behind them, Hillary at my side. I tossed her an annoyed look like, *What's wrong with this guy?* But she gave me an ambivalent smile in return.

We walked that way to the cafeteria, grabbed our bag lunches, and set off to find a shady spot to eat. We found it under a large, leafy tree and sat cross-legged in a tidy group.

"My head hurts from so many facts and figures," Hillary said and, as if to prove it, rubbed her temples.

"I'm not going to lie. I'm here for the hands on stuff," Bellamy said.

"Really," Curt drawled, tossing her a smile. "Me, too."

I was pretty sure I didn't like Curt. And I suddenly remembered that Bellamy did, that the reason she didn't want to be with him had nothing to do with not liking and everything to do with being afraid.

"I'm a little nervous about that part," Hillary said. "I mean, all those days in the wilderness with no shower or electricity?"

"If you didn't like it, why'd you come?" Curt asked her, downing a sip of his juice.

"I've been asking myself that since I arrived," she said grumpily, making me wonder if she was here for him, if she imagined this as their chance at love.

"Have you been camping before?" Curt asked, addressing Bellamy again, naturally.

"Yes," I answered for her. "We've been camping together. Lots of times. Which year was that your birthday sleepover?" I hadn't wanted to go because I thought it would be girl overload, but it had turned out to be fun. I remembered that Haven and I let Bellamy sleep between us. She said it was a Mulligan sandwich.

"My ninth," she replied. "The year of the Mulligan sandwich."

We shared a smile. It was odd how much history we'd had together without my notice. Until this trip, I wouldn't have put her on the list of people I was close to. But we had passed an entire lifetime together unnoticed.

"Maybe we should revisit the Mulligan sandwich," I said.

"We're missing half the bread," she said.

"We'll improvise," I said.

"What are you guys talking about?" Hillary asked.

"An inside joke," Bellamy said.

"You'd need years of longevity to understand," I added.

"We have nothing if not longevity," Bellamy added, pointing between us.

"I think maybe we have more than that," I said.

"Were we on the same car ride? Because if I remember correctly, you said…"

I picked up my cookie and shoved it in her mouth. "Shh, we're living in the moment, remember?"

She swallowed her bite of the cookie and held the rest to my lips. "Yes."

I ate the remainder of the cookie with my eyes on her, almost but not quite forgetting Hillary and Curt were still there.

They stuck with us until lunch was over and we all returned to class.

When class was over, I intended to spirit Bellamy away for our talk, but there was a group activity instead.

"Partner up," one of our instructors called. I saw Curt making a beeline for Bellamy.

You've got to be kidding me. It was time for drastic action, so I picked her up. "Mine." Curt blinked at me like maybe he finally understood I meant it for more than the game.

"Definitely seeing a whole new side of you," Bellamy said as she wriggled to get free. I set her down and she smoothed her hair, for all the good it did. Though it had started out lying nicely at the beginning of the day, now it was wild. I began to see why she usually wore it up. I watched, somewhat fascinated, as she pulled a band out of her pocket and attempted to fasten it.

"How so?" I asked, resisting the urge to reach out and help corral her hair.

"I've always thought of you as mild mannered. Haven is competitive and cutthroat, a firebrand, you know? I've always pictured you as the mellow twin. But maybe you're not."

I studied her, considering. I didn't know a man alive who wanted to be thought of as mild mannered. "Maybe I'm not." I gave up trying to resist and reached out with both hands, attempting to push the wayward hairs away from her face.

"My hair," she said, rolling her eyes. "It's an entity unto itself. Sometimes I think I almost hear it whispering to me."

"What's it saying now?" I gave up trying to tame her hair and rested my arms on her shoulders instead.

She stepped slightly closer and tugged my shirt. "It's saying, 'Who is this ridiculously nice looking guy, and why does he keep putting his hands on you?'"

"Does it want me to stop?"

"It's hair, Huntley. I didn't ask it because that would be weird."

"Hmm," I said. I was having one of those moments where everything seemed perfect and I wanted to stop time. They'd been happening the last year, as I sped closer to graduation and adulthood. It was as if I'd step outside myself and see the situation clearly and, like a narrator, a part of me would realize what was going on. *See that pretty girl in your arms? This could be the start of something big, of something special.* I had no idea where these sudden insights came from, or how I kept having them, but somehow I knew they were true.

"You keep looking at me like that. I'd love to know why," she whispered.

"Maybe sometime I'll tell you," I said. First I'd have to figure it out.

CHAPTER 8

It turned out that our pairing, while romantic, was not actually practical because we played one of those games where Bellamy had to hold on to my ankles and race me around like a wheelbarrow. She wasn't as slight and tiny as Haven, but she was much smaller than me, too small to effectively maneuver me around the playing field. We lost horribly, but it was fun.

"I hate losing," Bellamy said. We were sprawled out on the grass, our heads together, our feet apart, two parts of an unfinished triangle.

"Me, too," I agreed.

"What would Haven say if she were here?"

"I don't even want to imagine." My sister had a lot of great qualities. Losing graciously was not one of them. Neither was winning graciously, if I'm being honest. I didn't love to lose, but I didn't get as upset about it as she did. I was glad Bellamy didn't, either. I turned my head to look at her. She did the same, and we shared a smile. Her hand edged closer and our fingertips brushed, locking onto each other and joining.

"Hey," she said, and that one little word was enough to make my heart pound. *What is happening to me?* I wondered. I'd been with Bellamy in close proximity dozens and dozens of times over the years, in closer contact than this. We'd been sandwiched together in games of hide and seek, had fallen asleep in the back seat of our parents' vans, our heads lolling together, had shared opposite ends of the couch while watching a movie. Yesterday I drove her for three hours and didn't feel one trace of attraction to her, even when she rested her hand on my leg. And now...

"Hey," I said. "Do you have enough energy to take a walk with me?"

She took a breath, held it, and blew it out again. "Yes." We stood, brushed off our backsides, and headed toward the pond on the far side of campus, side by side but not touching.

We walked in silence for a while before I spoke. "I have something I need to say."

"So do I."

"You go first."

"You go first."

We stopped short and faced each other. "Count of three, we'll go together," She said. "One, two, three..."

"I think we should be together."

"I don't think we should be together."

"You don't think we should be together?" I said as her words registered.

"You think we should be together?" she added, then, "We're talking in circles."

I took her hands in mine. "I'll go. I think we should be together because, to my extreme shock and confusion, I think there might be something between us. We should see where it goes."

"I think we shouldn't be together because, to my extreme shock and confusion, I think there might be something between us. We shouldn't see where it goes," she said.

"But why? I don't understand." Even now, just holding her hands, staring at her face to face, I could feel it, this *thing*, this electrically charged something that was happening between us.

"I don't want to mess up our friendship, and what I said about Curt still counts."

I could feel my face scrunch into a grimace. "That guy. I don't get what you see in him."

She laughed a little and gave my hands a squeeze. "I don't mean because I like him. I barely know him. I mean it's the same because… because I'm afraid."

"Of me?" I asked, aghast.

She nodded.

I let go her hands and slid my arms around her, holding her gently. "Bellamy, come on. You've known me all my life. Don't you trust me?"

She had been staring at my chest. When she looked up, tears sparkled on her lashes. "I'm not ready for this, Huntley. I'm not ready for any of it. I thought I was, but I'm not."

She pressed her face to my chest and shuddered, trying to push back the tears. I hugged her tighter. This wasn't the Bellamy I was used to. That girl was irrepressible and never serious about anything. I wondered what had happened to make that one go away.

When she had herself back under control, she shifted, pressing her ear over my heart as her arms circled my waist, returning my hug. I rested my head on hers and eased my hand up and down her spine, feeling the tension drain out of her as I did so. It was a powerful feeling, like I was fixing whatever was wrong with her. I wanted more of it, not less.

"Hear me out," I began. "You're seventeen, almost eighteen. At some point you're going to get over this fear and be in a relationship. It's the nature of things. Why not with me, guy you know is safe?"

She eased away and peered up at me, the spark of amusement back in her expression. "You think you're safe?"

I nodded.

Her smile widened as her finger brushed my cheek. "Oh, Hot Huntley, you with the dancing and sweetness and charm. I think you might turn out to be the most dangerous one of all because I could love you. I could fall for you and lose my heart forever."

"Would that be so bad?" I whispered.

"Yes, because you might break my heart and then things would never be the same again. We could never go back to how it was before, when we were innocent of all the ways we could hurt each other."

"But then we'd also be innocent of all the ways we could make each other happy," I said.

She seemed to consider that. I pressed my advantage. "We promised not to overthink it this week. If it feels good, we're going to do it, remember? This feels good." I gave her a little squeeze. "Let's keep doing this."

"But it's us. Isn't it weird?"

"That's the thing, it's not."

"No, it's not," she agreed. "It feels natural, but also unexpected. How does a person you've known forever come out of nowhere?"

"Maybe some questions don't have answers, only solutions. Here's one thing I know for certain."

She looked up at me hopefully, expectantly.

"If Curt doesn't back off, I'm going to pound him."

She burst into a fit of giggles, and it felt like the sun eased from behind the clouds. My shirt was still clutched in her fists. She curled them tighter. "Are you ready for supper?"

"Yes." My thumb slid along her neck, tracing the faint outline of a delicate blue vein. I wanted to kiss her, but, given her fear, slower seemed better. She blinked up at me. For a moment, I struggled. The temptation to kiss her was almost overwhelming. But I had just given her a whole speech about trusting me, so I let her go and took a step back. "Let's go."

She smiled at me as if she sensed my struggle, as if she was feeling it, too. We set off together side by side. Our hands brushed and she linked her fingertips with mine. As before, my heart started to pound. I didn't know if it was this camp or this girl or this moment, but I knew something magic was happening. For now, that was enough.

CHAPTER 9

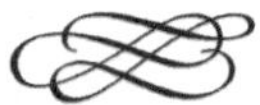

That night the pranks started. We ate supper with Curt and Hillary, who were apparently our new BFF's now, along with my roommate, Jeremy, and Bellamy's roommate, Fiona. Bellamy was back to being the bubbly extrovert I knew, and I was both relieved and puzzled by the contrast. How had I never noticed the other side of her nature before, the serious, tentative one? Probably in the same way I had never recognized her prettiness—because I hadn't been looking.

After supper we separated for a while. I played a game of Frisbee golf with some of the guys while Bellamy, Fiona, and Hillary hung out with a few of the girls. I was about to go to my dorm and shower when it occurred to me I needed to say goodnight to Bellamy.

This is me, checking in, being a good camp boyfriend who tells you goodnight.

A better camp boyfriend would do it in person, she replied.

I blinked at my phone, smiling. *That escalated quickly,* I replied and smiled wider as I imagined her laughing.

Easy, tiger. I just want to see you, to assure myself you're real and still alive.

Frisbee golf was brutal, but I made it. I sent her a fist bump emoji. She sent me praise hands in reply. And then I was standing in front of her dorm.

I kind of thought you'd be waiting for me, like a soldier returning from battle, I said.

Now I have to make it worth your wait. "Is that...?" I heard her yell and turned to look. She stood at the entryway of her dorm, eyes shaded with her hand as she stared at me. "Is that Huntley Mulligan?"

"It's me," I called.

She sprinted toward me, leaping at the last moment, forcing me to catch her as she wrapped her arms around me and clung. "My hero."

"You're really setting the bar high for greetings after this," I told her, but I didn't set her down.

"How was golf? Did you win?"

"It was good, I did not win."

"This is not your day for winning," she said.

"And yet I feel like a winner in this moment."

She grinned. "You get all the points for saying all the right things today."

"Yeah? What can I do with these points?"

"You accumulate them and use them to make purchases, like at Chuck E. Cheese," she said.

"What kinds of purchases?" I asked.

"I'm still setting up the store," she said, brushing her nose on mine.

"Wow, I have never been so excited to cash in before," I said.

"What do you think our moms would say if they could see us now?" she asked.

"Uh," I stammered. "That's not where I thought this conversation was going."

She laughed. "I'm serious. Do you think they'd be worried, shocked, enthused?"

I set her down but maintained my grip on her. "I think they'd tell us to be careful. But I think they'd also be cautiously optimistic."

"What a coincidence. That's also how I'm feeling at this particular moment," she said.

"I should go grab a shower," I said.

"You definitely should," she agreed.

"Does my stench offend you, Miss Brown?"

"I have four brothers, so I'm kind of used to stinky boys," she said.

"Yes, well I have three sisters, and I am still in no way used to soft, good-smelling girls," I said, burrowing my face into her neck. She giggled and tried to wrench away from me, but I held tight, biting her to make her laugh harder.

"Stop," she gasped.

I did because, being ticklish myself, I understood the torture.

"That was mean, and paybacks are no joke. You've been warned," she said.

I took in the sight of her wet lashes, flushed cheeks, and smile. "Totally worth it." I kissed her cheek and let her go. She took a step back, blinking at me in surprise. "I'll see you tomorrow."

"I'll make sure of it," she returned. "Thanks for stopping by. It was a very fake boyfriend thing to do."

"It was a real boyfriend thing to do, too," I said.

"Which one are you again?"

"Only history will tell." I touched my finger to the tip of her nose. "Go inside, I can't leave if you're still out here."

"You're very old fashioned. I like it." She kissed her finger and touched it to my cheek.

"Good, because it's probably not going to change anytime soon." I waited and watched until she was safely inside, and then I turned and walked back to my dorm. And that was when I realized that, while we were out playing Frisbee, the girls had raided our dorm and pranked us. They put Kool-Aid in the showerheads so that the first person who took a shower received a temporary dye job. They saran-wrapped the toilets and switched out the drawers in everyone's room so we spent a good hour tracking down everyone's items.

"Which one of them did it?" Jeremy demanded.

"Probably all of them," Ronan offered. "They're diabolical."

Secretly I knew that if Bellamy hadn't been the instigator, she had been the leader in at least most of the pranks. I knew too much about her and her family to think otherwise. But since my stuff was largely untouched, I didn't rat her out. And then I crawled into bed and realized she had short sheeted my bed. I fixed it and reached for my phone.

You're in trouble.

???

Nice try. You're forgetting Haven and I are the ones who taught you how to short sheet a bed.

Consider it an homage to good instruction, she replied. *Why are you still awake? I thought you were an early-to-bed type guy.*

Cleaning up the destruction you left in my dorm took longer than expected, I said.

Alleged destruction.

Thanks, counselor.

Good practice for when I'm actually a lawyer.

You want to be a lawyer?

How did you not know that? I've always wanted to be a lawyer, she replied.

Why are you at weather camp?

Stalking you, she replied. I considered that and discarded it. She could have stalked me at home for free.

Why really?

Looks good on college apps. Plus fun. I like science. #geekforlife

You'll be a great lawyer, I said and meant it.

Are you saying that because I'm good at arguing over nothing?

Among other reasons, I replied.

Now we have to get your career squared away. I vote doctor.

I couldn't tell if she was being serious or not. *Why?*

Because you'd be amazing at it. You're crazy smart but also have people skills and compassion. And all your patients would have crushes on you. Because hot.

It would require going away for college and med school, I said.

Going away is not your favorite. But a few years aren't so much, in the scheme of things. You could come home to set up practice. And it suits you.

What about the weather? I couldn't believe I was actually asking

Bellamy for future career advice, the topic that had been foremost in my mind the last two years.

The weather will always be there as a fun hobby, as it is now. Everyone needs a stress reliever. And don't forget the bees.

I don't think you'll let me.

Never. Why do bees stay in the hive in winter?

Do you want the real answer?

No. Because swarm.

audible groan

What's more impressive than a talking llama?

No.

A spelling bee. Why do beekeepers have such beautiful eyes?

Stop it, I'm begging you.

Because beauty is in the eye of the beeholder.

The more bee jokes you tell, the less I want to kiss you, I said.

Really?

...No.

So you do want to kiss me? she asked.

Was there some doubt?

Yes, because...you haven't.

Taking it slow seems best.

Right. But also? I want to kiss you, too.

There's always tomorrow.

Bet your bottom dollar.

I wish I didn't get that reference, I said. Unfortunately Haven went through a huge *Annie* phase where she made me watch it on repeat.

What did the bee say to the flower?

Ignoring you now.

Hello, honey!

I didn't reply. She waited a few minutes and texted again. *Hey, Huntley.*

This better not be for bee purposes, I warned.

Just wanted to say I had a good day with you and goodnight.

Same, and goodnight.

I thought that was the end, but my phone buzzed a few minutes later. *Want to know the best part of a bee's relationship? The HONEYmoon stage. That's where we are right now. XO.*

I set my phone aside and stared up at the ceiling, smiling. Then I reached for my phone and sent one last text.

What did the bee say to his girlfriend? You're a keeper.

She sent me a pink-cheeked emoji in return. This time when I set aside my phone, I fell asleep.

The next morning Bellamy was tardy for class again.

"What?" she mouthed when I gave her a look as she slid into her seat at the last possible second.

Since the instructor was already eyeballing us, I eased my notebook closer and wrote, *So late.*

So what? she replied.

So breakfast?

So not the time today.

So when? I asked.

So later.

So lying, I said.

She looked me up and down and responded, *So cute.*

So forgiven, I replied.

Smiling, she squeezed the back of my neck. My hand eased out and rested on her leg because suddenly I couldn't *not* touch her. Her hand covered mine. I adjusted our position, twining my fingers through hers.

I'm holding hands with Bellamy Brown. It was the first time we really held hands, apart from a friendly clasp. It was subversive and under the table, heightening the feeling for some reason. It was a good thing

I was a lefty and she was a righty, otherwise neither of us would have been able to write.

For that evening's activity, we went to a local lake to swim. "This makes me miss your pool," Bellamy said.

"Me, too," I agreed. I loved to swim, but swimming in a lake was another story. Still, it was a warm day and the water was cool. And Bellamy was in a swimsuit. Once again I was that guy, the one trying hard not to ogle. I didn't understand it. Bellamy and her family had been swimming at our house once a month for approximately forever, and I had never given her a second thought. But now, away from our homes and families, Bellamy and I were something different. We were seeing each other through new lenses. It was fascinating and exhilarating and scary, like slowly heading toward the top of a roller coaster. Only in this scenario I didn't know what was on the other side of the free fall.

We went our separate ways, she to the group of girls jumping off the dock and me to the group of guys playing water football. But I found my eyes straying to her more than once and a couple of times when I looked, she was looking at me, too. Eventually we migrated back together and sat drying out on the dock, our legs crossed and facing each other.

"I fear the smell of lake is never going to come out of my hair," she said, holding her hair aloft and sniffing it.

"It's not so bad," I assured her.

"That's because you smell like lake, too. We cancel each other out right now. But soon the differences between us will matter because you'll shower and smell good, and I'll shower and my hair will retain *au de* dead fish scent. And then it's going to matter. First you'll politely try to cover your nose when I'm not looking, and then you'll begin easing away, finding reasons to walk four feet apart. And then I'll die, a lonely fish scented old lady with nothing but cats for companions."

"Cats will love your smell," I said.

"I'm counting on it," she replied. She closed her eyes and tipped her face to the sun, smiling slightly. I watched, resisting the urge to reach out and touch her, to kiss her, to pull her close and hold her. She must have felt my eyes on her because she opened hers and looked at me.

"So many people around," I commented.

"Aren't there, though? You never realize how many people there are until you don't want there to be any," she said. Her finger reached out and trailed gently along my shin.

"I happened to notice that tomorrow night's schedule is listed as free time. A bunch of the guys are going out," I said.

"A bunch of the girls are, too. Did you want to go with them?"

"I was thinking maybe you and I could have our own outing," I said.

She tipped her head, studying me. "What sort of outing?"

"Sort of like a date." I reached for her hand and kissed her fingers. Her cheeks did that flushing thing I enjoyed so much.

"What would we do on this date?"

"Leave that to me," I said.

"You have no idea, do you?" she said.

"I'll figure something out. Did you bring a dress?"

She nodded.

"Excellent."

"I feel like I'm doing this all wrong," she said.

"Why?"

"Shouldn't I be playing hard to get, giving you the runaround, making you work for it and guess what I'm feeling and thinking?"

"While I do think the best relationships begin with cruel game playing, that doesn't seem like our style. But if it helps, I have no idea what you're feeling and thinking," I said.

"Well, then, at least I have that going for me," she said, giving me an enigmatic little smile.

"That was an invitation to tell me your thoughts and feelings, in case you missed it," I said, more than half hoping she would. I sort of figured she was attracted to me, but how much? Was this merely a camp thing for her? How did I compare to Curt, the guy she had initially secured for her camp fling? Were we interchangeable?

"Was it? Hmm." She lay down and stretched out. I followed suit until my phone buzzed with a text from Sutton.

How's Geektopia?

So far so good, I replied. When I finished, Bellamy was watching me curiously. "Sutton," I explained.

"That's Haven's boyfriend, right?"

"Yes, but we're good friends, too. He started out as my friend, actually."

"Do you have a picture?"

I hesitated. It wasn't a secret that girls found Sutton attractive, that if their reaction was any indication, he was better looking than I was. I hadn't given that a lot of thought before, mostly because the girl who liked him best was Haven. But did I actually want to show Bellamy his picture? Reluctantly, I pulled up a picture of Haven and Sutton together and handed it over.

Bellamy took it, squinting her eyes against the sun's harsh glare. She gasped. "Oh, my goodness."

I braced myself. "What?"

"Look how gorgeous and happy Haven is." She turned the phone toward me. I took it back, inspecting my sister. She did look almost supernaturally happy and pretty.

"I told you they have a good thing going," I said, more than a little relieved that she hadn't fawned over Sutton. My friends Reagan and Addison would have. Probably a reason I had never hooked up with Reagan and Addison, despite their repeated attempts. I had wondered if I was crazy for holding out and resisting them. I mean, I'll be honest, they're hot. But until now I didn't realize all the things they were lacking. Bellamy was pretty, but also smart and driven and funny and sweet and more than a little goofy and quirky.

"What?" she asked.

"What what?"

"You're staring at me," she said.

"Maybe I like what I see," I said and then because I couldn't resist any longer, I pressed my palm to her stomach, leaned closer, and brushed a soft little kiss against her lips, pulling back in time to watch my favorite little flush steal across her cheeks. It was like looking at a lava lamp, that flush; I could stare at it for hours.

"Where'd you come from, Huntley Mulligan?" she whispered.

"Turns out I've been here forever," I said. I lay down and took her hand, winding my fingers through hers.

CHAPTER 11

The next day I felt jittery and nervous, too much to even chastise Bellamy for her tardiness again. The little smile she gave me made me wonder if she felt the same. Tonight felt like a test somehow, a real date in the midst of whatever camp wormhole we'd entered. Camp was camp. Everything felt odd and different and full of possibility. But this would be an actual date, a chance to see if what was happening between us worked in the real world.

After class we separated, presumably so she could get ready. What did girls do that required ninety minutes of prep time? On my end, Jeremy, Curt, and I, along with a few other guys, played a pickup game of basketball. Fifteen minutes before it was time to leave, I grabbed a shower, got dressed, and walked to Bellamy's dorm. Her roommate, Fiona, was sitting outside staring at her phone. She looked up at my approach and whistled appreciatively.

"You clean up nice. Sure you don't want to take me instead?" she called.

I was pretty sure she was joking. So far everything I'd heard her say sounded like a joke, making her a good foil for Bellamy who was also rarely serious. "Better not let Bellamy hear you say that. She'll cut you. Girl's crazy."

"What girl's crazy?" Bellamy asked.

I looked up with a smile to answer, but it died as I stared at her, openmouthed. She had straightened her hair, a thing I didn't know was possible, given its immense amount of crazy curl. It hung to the middle of her back now, sleek and smooth and perfect. She wore a soft yellow dress, fitted to her waist and flaring softly to her knees, and I didn't think I had ever seen anyone look better.

Something clicked and I realized Fiona had taken a picture of my face, making me realize I had been staring for some time without speaking. I should say something clever or witty or at least flattering.

"Uh, wow," was what I came up with.

"Wow yourself," Bellamy said, smiling. "Nice tie."

"Ready?" Where had all my words gone? Why did my tongue feel ten times its normal size?

She nodded. "See you, Fiona."

"Hey you, lovebirds," Fiona replied. "Hold up." We faced her. She snapped another picture. "I'll send you that one."

"Thanks, Fi," Bellamy said, tossing her a little wave. I should probably thank her, too, but my words were still lodged somewhere deep, apparently. We walked in silence to my car. I held the door for her and closed it after she was safely inside.

Get it together, I coached myself. *It's just Bellamy.* I took a deep breath and slid behind the wheel.

"Feels weird, doesn't it?" she asked. "Like we're going to homeschool ball or something."

"No, it's way better than homeschool ball."

She laughed, "Yeah, you're probably right. Last year was terrible without you. I had no one to talk to. Did you go to homecoming?"

"I did. It wasn't all it was cracked up to be, either. Probably because my date ended up ditching me for my friend, Parker. But Sutton and Haven got back together, so it ended up okay."

"What about prom?"

"Prom was fun because I went with some of my friends, Parker and Addison and Reagan."

"Not Haven?"

"No, they couldn't decide if they were going to go with his friends or her friends so they went solo. But we all hung out after. It was fun."

"I went to prom," she said.

I darted her a look. "With who?"

"One of my friends named Dylan. I don't think you know him."

"Huh. So it was just a friends thing?"

She shrugged.

Not for the first time, I wished she came with a manual so I could decipher her words and gestures. "What does that mean?"

"He wanted to be more. I didn't."

"Why not?" I asked. *Please say it's because he's ugly with halitosis.*

"I wasn't ready," she said, turning to stare out her window.

"Oh." *Are you ready now? What became of him? Is he still in your life?*

She turned to me with a smile, resting her hand on my leg. "Thanks for this, Huntley. It's incredibly sweet. You're good at this."

"The night's young. Maybe you'll change your mind at the end of it," I said. I picked up her hand and kissed it. We were at a stop sign, so I was able to watch the blush spread over her cheeks until the car behind me honked.

"Not a chance," she said.

I kept her hand until we arrived at the restaurant I'd chosen. "I've never eaten Thai food before," she said.

"Me neither. I thought we could be adventurous together."

"Did I mention you're good at this?" she said, easing closer as she slipped her arm around my waist. I rested my arm on her shoulders and brushed my lips on her temple.

"For the record, your hair does not smell like lake."

"That's what every girl longs to hear from her fella," she said.

I didn't reply, mostly because I was happy to hear I was her fella. We placed our order and sat down to wait.

"Hey, Fiona sent me the picture of us." She turned her phone to face me. I took it and studied it closer.

"We look good together, like we belong, like we've always been doing this and it isn't our first date," I said.

"Excuse me, this isn't our first date," Bellamy said.

"What?" I asked, reluctantly handing her phone back. There was something compelling about the picture of us together, concrete proof that this was really happening.

"Don't you remember all the times we used to play house? Haven always made us be a couple, and she was always the restaurant owner where we came to dine. I distinctly remember several dates arranged by your sister where she fed us tea and animal crackers."

"I totally forgot about that, but you're right. This must be our twentieth fake date or something."

She sucked in a breath. "Wow, it's getting serious."

"I know. I should have gotten you a present. The twentieth fake date is kind of a big deal."

"Have you ever been on a twentieth date, for real?" she asked.

I shook my head. "I've been on a few dates. But nothing lasting. Nothing special." I reached for her hand, and I hoped she could understand what I didn't say. *Nothing like this. This is different; this is special.*

Our order was called. The remainder of supper was light and fun. We spent a long time talking about people we knew. Afterward, we went dancing.

"How did you find this place?" Bellamy asked, awed.

"It's my secret weapon. I call it Google. Don't tell anyone, though, because I'm trying to keep it to myself."

"Sounds like you're onto something there. What was it called again? Ogle?"

"No, but I think I've been doing that, too," I said, taking her hand to twirl her away from me. There wasn't a lot of room for conversation while we danced, but there didn't need to be. It was fun and casual and everything a first date was supposed to be.

"Do you have any plans for after?" Bellamy asked when it was time to call it a night.

"Walk you to your dorm?" I tried.

"I have another idea. Do you trust me?" She held out her hand for my keys.

"I trust you," I said, depositing the keys in her palm. She drove downtown, found parking on the street, and took my hand. We ascended a sharp rise that spilled out onto a tiny little park. Other couples were already present, sprawled out on the grass. We found a spot away from them and sat down.

"I wish I brought a blanket," Bellamy said, her tone regretful.

"Are you going to tell me what this is now?" I asked.

"Wait for it," she said. She stared at the horizon, along with everyone else. I stared, too. A couple of minutes later a giant firework lit the sky.

"Where is that coming from?" I asked.

"The baseball game just ended. They do it at the end of every home game," she said, leaning close to whisper. I eased my arm around her. She rested her head on my shoulder. The fireworks lasted about twenty minutes and were spectacular.

"I think those were better than what our town puts on for the fourth," I said.

"I agree, which is kind of sad for our town," she said.

We remained where we were a few moments, reluctant to break the mood. My hand made gentle little circles on her lower back, and I could feel her melt against me. *She likes to be touched,* I thought, filing the tidbit away in case I needed it later. Someday when she became angry with me, it would be good to have that ace in the hole. It was the perfect moment to kiss her, minus all the other people around us. Why was it so hard to find a moment alone?

"I guess we should get back," I said. I stood and put down a hand to help her up. She took it and sprang up lightly. We held hands all the way back to the car, walking in cozy silence. For my part, I felt a little dazed by the night's perfection. How was this all so easy and good? Wasn't it supposed to be harder than this? I started to open the car door for her, changed my mind, leaned her against it, and kissed her.

She kissed me back, standing on her toes to slide her fingers into my hair and tug me impossibly closer. I complied, pressing her into the car. We kissed for what felt like a long time but was probably only a couple of minutes, until a car horn blared, startling us apart. I rested my forehead on hers, trying hard to draw some much needed oxygen.

"I guess that answers that question," she said, sounding as shaky as I felt. "Turns out we do actually work together on all the levels."

"Pretty definitively," I agreed. I swallowed hard, resisting the urge to kiss her again. "We should get back."

"Probably," she said, as reluctant as I felt. "I wish it were possible to stay in this moment."

"I don't," I said.

She opened her eyes. "No?"

I shook my head. "Think of all the moments to come that we would miss," I said and, because I couldn't resist anymore, kissed her again.

CHAPTER 12

The date worked like flipping a switch between us. No more were we hypothetical or hovering in the realm of possibilities. We were authentic and truly together. It had all been so seamless that of course it couldn't last.

Camp was divided into two sessions. The first mostly involved class time, studying the history of weather, using calculations to make predictions. The second was the part I had most been looking forward to. We would transition to the weather observatory atop Mt. Washington in New Hampshire where we would stay for three nights, hiking and making field observations. I had been thinking a lot about what Bellamy said about my future career plans, and it made sense. In medicine, I could make a real difference. Meteorology could always be a fun hobby. The relief I felt at having made a decision was immense.

Two nights before the first part of camp was over, we had a giant bonfire, complete with hot dogs and s'mores. Bellamy and I sat at the edge of the circle, trying and failing to look like grownups as we ate our gooey marshmallows and melty chocolate.

"I give up. There is no good way to do this," Bellamy said, licking the tips of her fingers. "Did I get everything?"

She had a tiny dollop of chocolate on the tip of her nose. It was adorable. "Yep."

"Liar," she said, scrubbing her face with a napkin again.

"What makes you think I'm lying?" I asked.

"Because I know you."

"Baby, you're going to scrub your lips off," I said, reaching for the napkin. I took it out of her fingers, grasped her chin in my fingers and swiped the dollop of chocolate off her nose. When I finished, she was staring at me. "What?"

"You called me baby."

Now my cheeks flushed. I was glad for the cover of night to hide it. "Is that not okay?"

"It's okay. It's very, very okay," she said. Someone laughed nearby, breaking the spell, reminding us we weren't alone.

"So many people," I lamented.

"And yet some of them have no problem with an audience," Bellamy mused. We stared around the fire. More than half the current couples were involved in a full-throttle makeout session. We had an unspoken agreement to never be one of those couples, but I couldn't condemn them as much as I otherwise might have. It was harder than I imagined to find a quiet, private place to be alone. Unless we were willing to visit each other's dorm rooms, which we so far hadn't done. Other people were more than willing, however. Most nights played like a game of musical rooms.

"We might be the only virgins left standing by the end of camp," I whispered. Bellamy nodded and smiled. Across the fire, Jeremy caught my attention and signaled that he and Melanie were going back to our room. *Ugh.* This would be his fifth hookup since the beginning of camp, and I honestly didn't see the appeal. I turned to Bellamy to say as much, but she was sitting slightly hunched, her arms drawn tightly over her stomach.

"What's the matter? Are you sick?"

She nodded. "Too many s'mores. I think I might turn in. Sorry."

"Don't apologize. Can I get you anything? A soda or something?" I glanced around to see if there were any drinks left.

"No, I just need to go to bed." She dashed to her feet.

I stood. "I'll walk you back."

She put her hand out but didn't touch me. "No, you stay. Enjoy the fire a while longer."

I didn't say what I thought, that I wouldn't enjoy the fire without her. I didn't want to make her feel bad. But while I had been friendly with everyone, I had spent too much time with her to connect to anyone else. What's more, I didn't want to be with anyone besides her.

"I feel like I should walk you," I said. The campus seemed safe, but it was dark and she wasn't feeling well.

"It looks like Fiona's ready to go. I'll walk with her." She stood on her toes and kissed my cheek. "Night."

"Night," I said. My eyes followed her with concern. She didn't act like herself, but maybe it was as she said, she didn't feel well.

I sat and looked around for someone to talk to, but everyone was paired up. Going to my room was out because Jeremy was there. With nothing left to do, I wandered aimlessly around campus for a while, feeling lonely and forlorn. Nine days of being a boyfriend, and I was now that guy, the punchably pathetic kind who can't function without his girlfriend.

Eventually I wandered back to my dorm and knocked on the door. Melanie poked her head out, gave me a sheepish look, and skirted by me, eyes down. I didn't know exactly what went on in these situations, but I was fairly certain it wasn't Parcheesi. Jeremy went to take a shower. I readied myself for bed and vaulted into my bunk. I was about to text Bellamy when I received a text from her instead. I smiled in anticipation. It was her nightly routine to send me a corny bee joke. I pretended to hate them, but secretly I thought they were adorable. Last night's was still up on my screen. *What do you get if you cross a bee with a doorbell? A humdinger.*

My smile slipped as I read the new text.

I don't think I can do this anymore.

I sat up. *What? Why?*

For all the reasons I said before. Too much, too soon, too scary. Let's go back to the way it was.

I reviewed our evening together, but I couldn't fathom what had happened in the last few hours to scare her away, to make her change her mind. *I don't understand.*

I know. It's me. I'm kind of a mess. You've been amazing, but I just can't.

I need more than that. I wasn't sure what I meant. Did I need more explanation or more of her? Both things.

She didn't reply. In the morning, I was certain we'd get things straightened out. Face to face, I could talk some sense into her.

I didn't count on how thoroughly she would make certain I never got the chance.

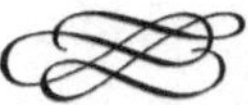

CHAPTER 13

Bellamy was predictably late for class. Unlike usual, she didn't slide into the seat next to me at the last minute. She sat at a table by herself in the back. Everyone's heads swiveled, looking between us.

I remained facing forward, stoic on the outside, shriveling on the inside. I missed her smell, her smile, her nearness, her lame excuses for why she was late. I missed her giving me a hard time for my promptness, my love of rules and order and breakfast.

What's a rule follower like you doing with a boho girl like me, she had asked more than once this week.

You're keeping me from being old and dull, was my standard reply, and it was true. I tended toward stability, security, status quo. Bellamy was my wildcard. She tended toward lateness and chaos and disorder, so much that even her hair couldn't be contained. By all rights it should drive me crazy. Logically, I shouldn't want anything to do with her. But there was no reason in romance, and I had never wanted anything more than I wanted her.

As soon as class ended, she disappeared. No matter how hard I tried, I couldn't pin her down. In desperation later that night, I texted the person who was now second on my list of favorites.

SOS

What's up? Haven replied.

I filled her in. It took her a few minutes to reply. *That doesn't sound like Bellamy. She's usually straightforward.*

I know. What should I do?

Give her time and space and try again. There was a pause and she wrote again. *You really like her, huh?*

I thought about the best way to explain it. *I think she might be to me what Sutton is to you.*

Wow.

I know.

I had just put down my phone when someone knocked on my door. I thought it was Jeremy. He had gone to another party in Cullen's room. It was a safe bet he would return too drunk to find his key.

But when I opened the door, I found Bellamy, a pillowcase over her head.

"What's up?" I said, aiming for casual. She didn't answer. I plucked the case off her head and realized she was bound and gagged, her face flushed with anger and embarrassment. I pulled her inside and took the tie off her face and hands.

"What's up?" I repeated.

She rubbed her wrists. The bindings hadn't been tight, but she seemed to need something to do with her hands. "Fiona, et al, decided to play matchmaker and force us together."

My heart turned over. *Thank you, Fiona.* "Yeah?" I smiled. She didn't.

"I can't."

We stared off until it became awkward. I wanted to force her to talk to me, but I didn't know how. I pressed my lips together to keep them from doing anything else, trying to cover my hurt and frustration. Where was my poker face when I needed it?

"Fine. I'll walk you home."

"Can't do that, either. They took my key and told me they won't let me in. Until morning."

"Oh." I pressed my lips together again, to keep from smiling this time. I had no doubt her friends meant it.

She blew out a breath. "I'll just sleep on the floor."

"No."

"What do you mean no?" she frowned up at me and even her frustration was cute.

"I mean I won't let you be in Jeremy's path when he stumbles in here drunk and stupid in the middle of the night."

"Oh," she said. She glanced at my bed and swallowed hard. "I guess we could each take an end, if that's okay. Like on the couch in your parents' basement."

I thought of that couch, of the many times I had laid there watching movies with Bellamy, of how I had never once reached for her, held her, kissed her. *So much wasted time.* "It's okay."

She vaulted onto the bed and curled onto the foot of it. I ascended more slowly, slid under the covers, and turned off the lamp.

We lay in silence a few minutes. She squirmed, contorting herself awkwardly around my feet and legs.

"Bellamy, this is crazy. You cannot curl up down there like an unwanted puppy. Come up here, please." I held the covers up for her. She must have been really uncomfortable because she didn't argue. Instead she got up, rearranged herself, and lay down beside me. We lay in heavy silence a few more minutes, the sides of our bodies feeling warm and tingly wherever they happened to touch. My heart thudded hard with repressed longing. The sweet scent of her tickled my nose until I thought I might actually die from the torture of it.

"Tell me what I did," I whispered. It wasn't the most suave opening, but I wasn't averse to begging at this point.

Abruptly she sat up and loomed over me. "Nothing. I told you, nothing. It's me. You were perfect. You *are* perfect."

Her hand reached out as if to touch my face but stopped short of its goal. For a second we stared at each other, and then it was as if someone dropped the match. I reached for her, pulling her impossibly closer, and then we were kissing.

After a few minutes one or both of us pulled away. She lay back down. I kept my eyes closed, sucking oxygen. I wanted to kiss her again. More than that, I wanted to understand. I took her hand, winding my fingers through hers. "Please talk to me, please."

She took a shaky breath. "I can't."

"Why not?"

"Because you probably won't like me anymore if I tell you."

I wanted to assure her that of course I would, but the weight of her tone gave me pause. If it was something she considered so monumental, it would be unfair of me to dismiss it so easily. "Trusting me means taking a step out onto the bridge. If I let you down, then that's on me. But if you never give me the chance, that's on you."

She took a couple more shaky breaths and clutched my hand so tightly it hurt. "The thing you said about the flannels, that was true. You know I was a total tomboy. And then the year I turned thirteen, suddenly I was a girl. But I didn't feel like a girl. Growing up the way we did, I was so sheltered and innocent. That summer, when I was thirteen, I went to camp." Her voice was shaky and soft, as if the words were hard. Her hand was steady in mine, but her body trembled. I longed to hold her, but for the moment I made myself lie perfectly still, listening.

"I wasn't into boys yet. The day before I left, I played Barbies for three hours. Then I got to camp, and all anyone could talk about was boys. One boy in particular started to pay me a lot of attention, and for the first time I began to see what all the fuss was about.

"That first night he asked me to take a walk with him. We went somewhere private, and he kissed me, my first kiss. He told me how special I was, how beautiful, how interesting and wonderful. He told me I was the most amazing and awesome girl at camp, that he wanted me to be his girl. Only we had to keep it secret because..." She faltered, swallowed, and tried again. "Because he was a counselor."

"How old was he?" I tried to keep my tone neutral, but my hand, the one that wasn't holding hers, was squeezed into a fist.

"Twenty seven. I didn't know that then. I thought he was the age we are now, that he was maybe in high school or college. He seemed a lot younger. The week progressed, and so did the encounters with him. By the end of camp..." She trailed off and stared away from me, toward the door. I uncurled my fist and used that arm to drape over her waist, giving her a hug while still holding her hand.

She took a deep breath and tried again. Her words were softer this time, harder to hear. "Last night when you said that thing about us being the only virgins here…I just…I'm not that person, not the person you think I am."

I took a minute to answer because I wanted to get it right, so badly didn't want to mess it up and make it worse. I rolled toward her, let go of her hand, and embraced her with both arms, drawing her tight against me. "Bellamy, I'm so, so sorry you had to go through that. And I'm so sorry you read anything into my words more than the flippant statement they were. But, baby, this isn't the fifteenth century. You are not judged on your virginity. You are everything, and I care about you so much. Nothing is going to change that, not the actions of some… What happened to him, by the way?"

Her face was pressed to my chest, her arms clutching at my waist. She took a minute to get herself back under control. I smoothed my hand over her head, and that seemed to help. She wasn't crying, but she was trying hard not to.

"A few months after camp, I had a breakdown and told my parents everything. I was so confused. In my mind, he and I had a relationship. It's taken a few years of therapy to be able to see it clearly, to be able to understand that he preyed on me, groomed me, used my innocence against me. I had no idea, none. I was so clueless, and he led me along with such skill…When my parents found out, we made a police report. There was an investigation, but it was my word against his. We ended up coming to some sort of middle ground. There was no trial, no arrest and prosecution. In exchange, he promised to never work with youth again and, obviously, to stay away from me forever." She shuddered.

"I'm so sorry," I repeated. "It kills me to think he's out there, roaming free somewhere."

She nodded against my chest. Her hand smoothed along my ribs, my fingers sifted her hair. "Huntley."

"Hmm."

"Thank you."

"For what?"

"For believing me. I've never told anyone besides my parents before. It's…not easy, carrying the knowledge, the guilt, the shame, the memories and remorse. Knowing how much he stole from me, the things I can never get back." She started to cry then, soft, gentle tears. It felt like something she had probably cried over before, many times, as if these tears were a return to something unfinished, something that might always remain undone.

"I know all of that's true, Bellamy. But there are some things he'll never be able to take from you, so many more firsts left to experience," I said. I turned my head to look at her. She tipped her face toward mine and swiped her eyes.

"You make me believe that," she whispered. "I'm sorry I pulled away. I freaked out. Not the first time, probably not the last."

"I'm fine with the freaking out. Just take me with you next time."

She smiled and sat up slightly. I remained frozen as she eased closer, took my face in her hands, and kissed me. It was a different sort of kiss, less frenzied and passionate, more tender and slow. But it had the same effect on me, a mix of pleasure and pain that started in my stomach and spread outward. One of my hands tangled in her hair while the other spanned the small of her back, drawing her impossibly closer. She obliged, her fingers easing onto my scalp, twining into my hair as she kissed me again and again.

The door burst open and Jeremy entered, belting a Bruno Mars song. We froze, but he didn't turn on the light. Drunkenly, he gathered his supplies and headed back out, toward the bathroom. Bellamy and I let go of each other. She lay down, resting her head on my shoulder.

"Those are definitely not the right lyrics," she whispered. For some reason it struck us both as being incredibly funny. We laughed until tears streamed down both our cheeks. I reached out to swipe at her wet cheeks and she did the same to mine. She clasped my hand and rested her head on my shoulder again.

"You know what this feels like?" she whispered.

"What?"

"Feels like forever." The weight of the words hung between us. I picked up her hand and kissed the back of it.

"Feels like the beginning."

"That, too," she agreed. She slung her arm over my waist, snuggled closer, and we both fell asleep.

CHAPTER 14

The next morning we loaded a bus, very bright and very early. It would be a long day of driving to get to New Hampshire. As much as I wanted to get there, I found I didn't mind the drive so much. Maybe it was the sleepy girl now curled in my embrace, her hair still wet from the shower, her face still free of makeup.

At a rest stop a couple of hours in, she finally perked up and emerged wearing makeup, her hair piled in some intricate updo that was already coming loose.

"How do girls do that?" I asked.

"Use the bathroom? It's basic biology," she said.

"Change everything so easily and quickly. It's like magic," I said, waving my hand toward her face and hair.

She wrinkled her nose. "I don't usually let guys see the 'before' me, but you've kind of grown up with it, so…"

"Lucky me," I said. "For the record, I like the before as much as the after."

"Sweet liar," she said, brushing her nose on mine.

I kissed her. The seats were tall and we were scrunched low, hidden and cocooned in our own bubble of intimacy. But I didn't care anymore. I just needed to kiss her in that moment.

"Hey, Huntley," she whispered when the kiss was over. Her finger skimmed my face, making me feel drowsy.

"Hmm."

"How do bees get to school?"

"No," I said. "Stop it."

She leaned closer, her lips almost but not quite touching my ear. "The school buzz."

"You're ridiculous." I said, but I eased my arms around her and gave her a squeeze.

"I was so excited about this leg of the trip—Mt. Washington, the hiking, the roughing it. But this," she pointed between us, "supersedes all of that. I'm pretty sure we could be in a windowless room, staring at a cinderblock wall and still have fun."

"I would welcome being stuck in a windowless cinderblock room with you right now," I said as someone walked down the aisle, jostling into me.

"Oh, man," she mashed her hand over her eyes. "Think what it's going to be like at home with our combined fourteen siblings streaming in and out. 'Bellamy, why are you kissing Huntley? Why is Huntley kissing you? *Ew.*'"

"Please tell me you were not the one saying 'ew' in that scenario," I said.

"Seriously, it's going to be a nightmare."

"After watching Sutton and Haven this year, trust me when I tell you there are definite ways of finding alone time. We'll have to be ingenious and sneaky."

"You be ingenious; I'll be sneaky," she said.

"Boom, done," I said, giving her a fist bump.

Her phone buzzed with a text. Smiling, she answered it before tucking her phone away. "Your mom?" I guessed.

"No, that was Dylan."

"Prom Dylan?" She nodded. "You guys text often?"

"I told you we're friends." She cocked her head, studying me. "Are you jealous?"

"No. A little. A tsunami amount." I had never been jealous of anyone before. It wasn't a pleasant feeling. "Do you have a picture?"

"How did you not see pictures of us from prom? My mom plastered them all over social media," she said as she scrolled through her phone in search of a picture.

"We weren't exactly paying attention to each other before this trip," I said as she handed me her phone. I had hoped that Dylan would turn out to be like most of our homeschool friends—homely and nonthreatening. But he wasn't. If he went to my school, we'd likely be in the same group, and I could only imagine what Addison and Reagan would say.

"Did you kiss him?" I asked.

"Do you really want an answer to that question?" she said.

I nodded.

"Yes. We made out for a bit. Didn't stick."

"Bad kisser?" I asked.

"No, I just," she frowned at her phone, thinking. "I don't know. It didn't click or something. Every time I tried to like a guy, I'd get scared or old memories would resurface and I'd feel like I was having a panic attack. Until you." She put down the phone and looked at me. "You circumvented my fear factor because I already knew and trusted you. I did not see you coming; it was the perfect sneak attack."

"Relationship ninja skills for the win," I said.

She smiled at me, tracing her finger over my face again. "What you said before, it wasn't completely true."

"Which part?" It was hard to think clearly when she was touching me like that. Or touching me at all, really.

"I definitely noticed you before this trip, and I was only half joking in the car on the way here. I started noticing your cuteness a couple of years ago. I've had a low-level crush on you since then."

"Why didn't you say something?"

"It was obvious you weren't into me, and I didn't really want it to advance. You were pleasant to look at, to think about. I didn't really need or want it to be anything more."

"But think of all the fun we've been missing out on the last couple of years. I could have taken you to homecoming and prom. I could have saved you from the world's worst kisser, Dylan."

"I think this, right now, is the perfect time for us. Who's to say it would have worked out for us two years ago or last year or even last month? Things happen when they happen for a reason."

"You're such a flower child," I said.

"And you're so prescriptive. Someday it's likely these differences between us will drive each other insane."

"Who says they don't now? You annoy me greatly," I said, pressing my face to her neck and inhaling. I had no idea if it was something she wore that smelled so good or her natural scent. Whatever it was, I couldn't seem to get enough of it.

"Back at you," she said.

We stopped for supper but didn't venture out of our happy bubble to eat with anyone else. Camp was winding down. I wondered if Bellamy felt as anxious as I did about returning to the real world. How would things translate back home? Would they? Did she want them to? In the beginning, we said this was going to be fake, but that proved untrue. Then we said it would be only for camp. That wouldn't hold, either, would it? Soon we needed to have a talk about that. For now I wanted to enjoy the time we had left, as much as we could. The next few days would be physically assaulting. There likely wouldn't be a lot of time or energy leftover for anything else, even romance.

We arrived in New Hampshire at night, too late to do anything else but unpack and settle in. As soon as we stepped off the bus, I felt the change in temperature and wind velocity, resisting the urge to shiver as I unloaded our bags and carried them to our bunk.

Unlike at the college where we'd been, the weather observatory was much smaller and more primitive. There were two very small rooms for us to stay, one for girls and one for guys, with a row of bunk beds and not much else. There was a small communal living room and kitchen. Bellamy and I unloaded our luggage, made up our beds, and met back in the living room.

"We have an early day tomorrow, guys. I'm instituting a curfew tonight. You have one hour until lights out," our instructor, John, told us. No one complained because we were all excited for the next day's adventure.

"Let's go outside," Curt suggested.

Mt. Washington was the ideal place for weather camp because it is one of the windiest places on earth with an average wind speed of 32 miles per hour. It also held the record for the highest wind speed ever recorded by man at 231 miles per hour. We all hoped for a storm to experience some of the wind and rapid weather changes, sort of like going to a hockey game and hoping for a fight.

We had put on our jackets, but it was still a chilly 40 degrees out, despite the fact that it was July. This morning when we left the school, it had been eighty. The wind now was around forty miles per hour, blustery but not impossible. It was enough to tug Bellamy's hair free of its restraint and force it to whip around her face. She had to keep letting go of me in order to push it back. Laughing, I gathered it up in both my hands and held it for her, giving her a reprieve from the repeated lashings. She stood on her toes and burrowed her cold face into the crook of my neck. I let go of her hair and wrapped both arms tightly around her, warming her.

"You're good for all the things," she said, practically yelling to be heard over the beating wind. In answer, I kissed her. The darkness was a good cover. Who knew when we'd get the chance again? We kissed for a few minutes, until the wind worked her hair between our faces, tickling us and getting in between our lips. We pulled away, laughing and batting our faces.

We walked inside and said goodnight soon after, but my phone buzzed with a text as soon as I was in bed.

Is it pathetic to say I miss you?

Completely. And I miss you, too. Completely. The sooner we go to sleep, the sooner it will be tomorrow.

YES. Goodnight. PS. Why do bees have sticky hair?

Pretending this isn't happening now, I typed. But I was not disappointed when she sent one more reply.

Because they use honeycombs.

I planned to ignore her but couldn't. I sent her a smile emoji. She sent me a heart in return and we fell asleep.

CHAPTER 15

"Let the record show I made it to breakfast," Bellamy whispered. It was so early in the morning whispering seemed the only appropriate form of communication.

"Totally worth the wait," I said, leaning forward to give her a quick kiss.

"If I'd known it would involve kissing, I might have shown up before now," she said.

"Really?"

"*No*," she mouthed, shaking her head. Despite the fact that she hated breakfast, she ate a substantial amount, a nod to all the physical work we'd be doing in the hours to come.

"You look adorable," I said. I had already finished eating and had nothing to do but sit and stare at her. She wore one of her old flannels, making me realize she hadn't been wearing them since camp began. I wondered if maybe that was because of me, because being with me made her feel comfortable with her body. Or maybe safe and protected. I hoped she felt that way. I got a little gooey staring at her, thinking about stuff.

"It's not awkward at all that you're staring at me as I shovel oatmeal," she said.

"I've turned into a complete and total loser," I mused. "Seriously. I never thought I would be that guy who stares at a girl because she looks so incredibly cute while drinking coffee, but here I am."

"Here we both are," she said, reaching out to touch her palm to my cheek.

"You ready for today?"

"Ready and enthused. And it turns out that last night's walk was educational because I realized the need for a headband." She tapped the wide swath of fabric now trying valiantly to contain her hair.

I plucked at it, testing the elastic. "How long do you think that will last?"

"Between my hair's freakishly strong will and the wind's power, I'm giving it four hours."

"I say three. I've seen what your hair can do."

"Care to make a wager?" she asked.

"Someone betting?" Fiona said. "I want in on that."

"Me, too," Curt piped up.

Soon everyone in our group had placed a bet on Bellamy's headband, so many we had to write it down to keep track. The most optimistic was our instructor, John, who thought the headband would hold all day. The least was Hillary who gave it an hour.

After breakfast we were ready. Everyone was in high spirits. The hike was listed as moderate, meaning we didn't need gear to complete it, only a high level of energy and good health. The day was supposed to be partly cloudy. At the moment it was foggy, so foggy it was impossible to see more than a few feet in front of us. The trail was clearly marked, but our progress was slow until the sun fully rose, burning off a bit of the fog. Like the night before, the wind was intense, keeping steady at around 35 miles per hour with occasional gusts.

Bellamy and I hiked side by side in silence. She was in good shape and fairly athletic, but also shorter. Occasionally I offered her a hand up, and she took it, tossing me a smile.

"Perfect day," I commented.

"Absolutely."

I was glad she didn't feel the need to fill the space between us with incessant chatter, especially when there was so much nature to enjoy around us. This was my element—being outside, connecting with the earth, able to breathe free and think clearly.

"We should do this more often," Bellamy said softly and I smiled, glad we were on the same page.

"For sure," I agreed. We were on a relatively level portion of the trail for a bit. I reached for her hand and gave it a squeeze. She squeezed mine in return. As with everything else with her lately, the moment felt perfect. I wanted to bottle it. At the same time, I began to trust the perfection. Maybe these moments weren't blips. Maybe this was the new normal. Maybe this was how it would always be with her, easy and natural and amazing.

We broke for lunch and were getting ready to head back when one of the fast weather changes happened in an instant. This was what we were here for, but it was different to read about it and experience it firsthand.

The wind increased, gusting between fifty and sixty miles per hour. A quick glance of the barometer on my watch told me a storm was coming, but I didn't really need the watch because I was seeing it in real time. John, our instructor, who was used to the mountain's rapid weather changes, told us to take off our backpacks and anything metal on our bodies. He had to shout to be heard over the rushing, swirling wind. Quickly, we shrugged out of our packs and piled them a safe distance away. Metal zippers counted, too. The one on my jacket was plastic, but a few people had to take off their coats, weathering the now icy air with shivers. Bellamy had it worse than that, though. Her arms pulled into her shirt, she made a few contorted movements, and a moment later slipped off her underwire bra. I turned away, my cheeks flushing. If I'd known that was what she was doing, I wouldn't have watched. Probably.

We finished de-metalling ourselves as the first streaks of lightning began to shoot off in rapid succession.

"Assume the position," John called, or at least that was what it looked like he said. I could no longer hear him. But when he dropped into a crouch on the balls of his feet, covering his ears and closing his eyes, the rest of us followed suit. I waited to close my eyes until I saw that Bellamy was safe, and she did the same to me, tossing me one last smile as she tucked her head into her chest.

And then the lightning began in earnest.

I had always loved storms. Some of my earliest memories include pressing my face to the window to watch it rain, blow, hail, and storm. But being safe inside a house was far different than being on the side of a mountain. This time I could *feel* the lightning. There was so much static in the air my hair stood on end. I could feel the heat, strange shots of fire splitting the cold wind and rain now swirling around us, like splotches of warmth amid the cold. And even with my hands pressed over my ears the sound of thunder seemed to echo to the center of my brain. If it had merely been me, I wouldn't have worried, but now I worried for Bellamy. Being struck by lightning was a real possibility. Death had never felt so near before.

Eventually, the storm ended. I opened my eyes, looking first to Bellamy who was looking at me.

"*Okay?*" she mouthed.

I nodded. "*You?*"

She nodded. We scanned the rest of our group. Everyone looked unscathed. We unfurled ourselves from our crouches and began sorting the sodden pile of backpacks and jackets.

"Bellamy, I think this is yours," Curt said, holding her bra aloft with a smile. Since I was closer, I snatched it away from him and realized it wasn't much better that I was now holding it. It dangled on the tip of my finger as Bellamy reached for it.

"This has been the most awkward storm of my life," she said.

"Definitely the most interesting one of mine," I agreed.

"Can I trust you to keep watch for me while I go over there and put this on?" she asked.

"Scout's honor," I said, raising my hand.

"You were never a scout," she said.

"Then I guess you'll just have to trust me," I said.

"That would easier to do if you weren't actually leering at me right now," she said. She shucked out of her jacket and disappeared off the trail for a moment. Dutifully, I turned my back on her and kept watch, though no one attempted to bother her. She reappeared a minute later and took her jacket back. "Would it be whiny to say I'm freezing?"

"No, I'm freezing, too. But soon we'll be back at the observatory. We'll find a blanket and snuggle up together with cocoa."

"It's cute how you have that dream scenario going on when, in reality, we'll be sardined in the common room with everyone else, struggling to find a chair or moment of silence. Also, by the time we get back, it'll be way too warm for a fire."

"Shh, let me have this moment. It's all that's keeping me warm," I said.

"You've got it," she agreed.

By the time we returned back to the observatory, we had dried out. But in the interim we had spent the entire day hiking while wet and cold. When supper rolled around, we were all exhausted. We had to take turns with the shower in batches. Bellamy was in the first batch, and I was in the last. After we finished and met back up in the common room it was predictably crowded and there was no fire, blanket, or cocoa to be found. We huddled together in a little corner, leaning against the end of the couch. I slid my arm around her. She snuggled into me. A few minutes later, she was asleep.

Despite the exhaustion, the lack of comfort or privacy, it was the perfect end to a perfect day.

CHAPTER 16

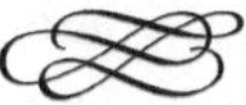

The next day was spent at the observatory. We took a tour, talked to the on-staff meteorologists, and helped take daily measurements of the instruments. It was fascinating, but I felt surprisingly removed from it, as if I had already found a benediction on something that had been a part of my life for as long as I could remember.

I don't ever remember not wanting to be a meteorologist. In contrast, medicine was a new venture. Last year was my first biology class and my first dissection. It had deepened my interest in the subject, but I still thought meteorology would win. And now that it hadn't, I was both shocked and relieved. It felt good to have a definitive answer, but I also felt a bit nostalgic over the loss of something that had been a big part of my life forever.

"Why do you look so sad?" Bellamy whispered during a pause in the tour.

"I'm saying goodbye to the weather," I whispered, and it was indicative of my trust in her that I didn't hesitate over the odd statement.

"I'm sorry," she said, giving me a sweet smile. "Are you certain?"

"I'm certain," I said with a definitive nod. "Once I make up my mind on something, there's no going back."

"That's what I'm counting on," she said, giving my sleeve a little tug.

I got caught up staring at the back of her as she walked away, a stupid grin on my face. There wasn't another way to interpret that, was there? She had been making a statement on us, hadn't she?

The next morning we set off at dawn for another long drive back to the college where we'd been staying. Once again Bellamy was sleepy, but this time I was, too. We both slept a few hours, until we reached our first stop. As before, she emerged from the bathroom looking like a new creation, bright eyed and beautiful, while I remained travel worn and gritty.

"You're putting me to shame here," I said, attempting to smooth down my hair.

"You're doing fine," she assured me, patting my stomach.

On the second leg of the journey we talked about what the upcoming year would be like. She only had a few classes left to take to meet her graduation requirements, and since I was already done, we'd both have a lot of time to work and save money for the next year.

"It's going to be a weird year," she said, and I agreed.

"Like being in limbo," I said, though now that I had a concrete life plan, I felt better than I had before. At least I had a goal to work toward. At least now I knew better which colleges to apply to.

"It's going to be like being an actual grownup, in a way. We'll be working, saving, making real life decisions about our future. It's kind of a big deal," she said.

"Except we'll still be living at home, still not have bills to pay," I said. "It's like a practice run for real life."

"You sound alarmingly stable and well-prepared," she said.

"I'm not," I assured her. "I've been dreading this year since I first became aware of it. The first night Haven mentioned going away to college, I actually threw up. I went to public school last year, mostly so we could have more time together, more memories and experiences.

I've tried to figure out a way to stop time with no success. But now that it's here..." I broke off, shrugging.

"What?" she prompted. "You're magically okay with your twin and best friend going away?"

"No, but...For so long I felt like I would be alone when Haven left. I mean, I realize how stupid that sounds because I have seven siblings. But it's not the same as it is with Haven, you know? The two of us have always been a pair. Without her, I'm outside of everyone else. But I didn't foresee that something else might come along."

"What?" she said, her face a total blank.

I laughed. "You can't possibly be as obtuse as you're pretending to be. You. I'm talking about you."

"Oh," she drawled, the pretty flush stealing over her cheeks. When she otherwise didn't respond, I began to backpedal.

"That is, I mean, if you still want to do this when we get home. We said it was going to be for camp, and I..."

She interrupted me in the best possible way, with her lips on mine.

"So that's a yes, then," I said.

"That's a definitely and completely yes. I don't want this to end, Huntley."

"Me, neither," I said.

"I didn't know that was actually a possibility anymore, us ending. And now that I know you were thinking about it, I'm wondering if I was supposed to," she said.

"No, because I wasn't thinking about it. I was thinking about ways to talk you out of it," I clarified.

"You're so adorably good at saying all the right things at the right time," she said.

"When we get home, I'm only going to have a couple of weeks until Haven and Sutton leave for school."

"I understand. You're going to need some time and space."

I rolled my eyes. "It's like you're misconstruing my words on purpose. I meant it only gives us a short window to hang out with them as a couple."

"You want me to intrude on your last few days with them?"

"No, I want you to save me from being a third wheel for once. It's always them and me. You have no idea how lonely that gets."

"What if they don't like me?" she asked, and I laughed.

"You've known Haven as long as you've known me."

"Yes, and until very recently I was not on your list of favorites. I doubt kissing Haven will make her feel differently about me," I said.

"Haven has always liked you, will continue to like you. And Sutton doesn't care what happens around him, so long as Haven is happy. He's pretty whipped. It's kind of pathetic." Actually, it was kind of how I was, and I got it now. My priorities had re-centered on Bellamy. If she was smiling, it was a good indicator I'd be smiling, too. Fortunately for us both, she was usually happy-go-lucky and easy to please.

"Do you think this is so easy because we're both middle children from big families?" Bellamy asked.

"Maybe it won't always be this easy. Maybe it's only easy because it's new," I said.

"Don't be pessimistic, Huntley. And maybe it's easy because it's meant to be, did you ever think about that?"

"No. Not to bring down your romantic moment or whatever, but I don't believe in destiny."

"Then how do you explain both of us being at that camp at the same time?" she asked.

"Our moms are best friends. My mom told your mom about the camp and your mom told you."

She blew out an exasperated breath. "That is so irritatingly practical."

"But no less untrue."

"What if we didn't get together because our moms were friends? What if our moms became friends because we were destined to be together?" she countered.

I picked up one of her curls, watching it sift through my fingers and bounce back. "You're such a flower child."

"What's wrong with that theory?" she demanded.

"Love is a matter of accessibility. It's scientific fact that people fall for the people they spend the most time with," I said.

"Or do they happen to spend time together because they were already predestined to be together?" she said.

I shook my head. "It's all about proximity."

Frowning, she yanked her curl free of my fingers.

I sat up from my slouch. "You're not actually upset about this, are you?"

"Upset? Why would I be upset? Because my boyfriend believes I'm replaceable with any other girl who has *proximity*?"

"But so am I. I could be some other guy. Serendipity doesn't exist in real life."

Her jaw dropped and her arms flung out in full Bellamy drama. "Of course it does."

With effort, I suppressed my amusement, a difficult feat because she was so stinking adorable. How had I ever cringed away from her passionate nature when now I couldn't get enough of it? "Of course it does not. That's what makes books and movies so great, because they're serendipitous. But in real life there are no meet-cutes, no happy resolutions. Nothing fits with such tidy endings. Real life is a little bit of chance and a whole lot of messy."

"That doesn't bother you?" she said, aghast. "The thought that we're some guy and some girl who are together because we spent enough time in each other's *proximity*."

"No, because it's not some other girl or some other guy. It's you and it's me. Who cares how or why it came about? Can't we enjoy the fact that it did?"

I could tell she relented, but I could also tell the discussion wasn't completely over, it was merely postponed to a later time. Maybe this was how real relationships worked. Instead of breaking up over every stupid argument, you put them on the back burner—to solve later. Or to realize they weren't important enough to solve?

"How can you be so sweet and romantic and thoughtful and frustratingly pragmatic all at the same time?" she asked, grasping my shirt to give me a little shake.

"Layers, baby," I whispered close to her ear and was rewarded when she gave a little shiver. Despite her skewed reasoning, she wasn't purely a hippie. She could be driven and focused and competitive, could be ruthless, if she believed she was right, whereas I lacked the killer instinct almost completely.

"We complement each other in all the ways," I mused out loud, sounding as startled by the revelation as I felt. When would being with her stop taking me by surprise? The ease, the rightness, they felt too good to be true. Soon I would learn perhaps they were.

But when Bellamy leaned closer to murmur against my lips, "That's because we have such strong *proximity,*" I forgot everything but her.

CHAPTER 17

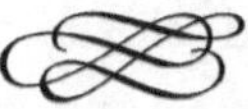

We returned to the college late that night, and still Bellamy and I had a hard time saying goodnight.

"I can't believe it's over," she said, her words muffled against my chest. We weren't doing anything besides hugging, but it felt safe and warm and perfect and neither of us ever wanted it to end.

"Don't say it like that. You make it sound permanent. It was camp. We're not over; we'll still be together." I rubbed a comforting little circle on her back, drawing my own comfort from her softness pressed against me.

"Yes, but it won't be the same, will it?" She pulled back slightly to see my face. "Being together every minute at camp, eating all our meals together, being alone together among so many strangers. It forced a special kind of intimacy, accelerated the timeline of our relationship. I mean, without camp we likely would have been on one, maybe two dates by now. With camp we've had fourteen solid days of togetherness. We're at, like, the four month mark in real time or something."

It was a fascinating glimpse into how girls' minds worked. I hadn't thought of any of this stuff. To me, it had been fun to be together. Beyond that, I hadn't given things a lot of consideration. But Bellamy had assigned meaning and length to our relationship, had already categorized it in her head and in her heart.

"Why are you looking at me like that?" she asked, her tone wary.

"Like what?" What did my face look like when it looked at her? I had no idea.

"Kind of dreamy, kind of amused."

"Because I find you dreamy and amusing. See also: beautiful, adorable, and funny."

Smiling, she pressed her ear over my heart. "I guess I should go in."

"Will I see you at breakfast tomorrow?"

"You are obsessed with breakfast," she said.

"Yes, truly it is breakfast that obsesses me," I said, giving her a squeeze.

"I will see you at breakfast," she promised and stood on her toes to give me a quick kiss. She started to pull away but I pulled her back and kissed her again. We rested our foreheads together.

"Maybe it's a little harder to end camp than I thought it would be," I admitted.

She smiled and tapped my chest. "I knew you had a heart in there somewhere, Tin Man." She gave me one more kiss and walked away while I stood on the sidewalk, forcing myself not to call her back.

The next morning we were quiet at breakfast, both of us feeling a bit melancholy and trying to hide it. We said goodbye to everyone else and loaded our belongings into my car. We drove in silence a few minutes until I couldn't take it anymore.

"It's going to be fine."

"I know it is. We're going home, not breaking up."

I shuddered. "Don't even say that."

"Why, you think saying it is going to make it happen? That's a superstitious belief from Mr. Logical." She poked me.

"It's not superstition. I just don't like hearing the words."

"You mean you don't like me putting them into the universe because that could make them come true," she said.

"No, that's ridiculous. They make me uncomfortable because they're ugly words."

"Ugly words? Wow."

I poked her. "Hush, you."

"All I'm saying is that I think you're more of a hopeless romantic than you think you are," she said.

"I'm really not. Sorry, not sorry."

She pursed her lips, crossed her arms, and looked out her window.

"Uh-oh," I muttered. "Can't we agree to disagree?"

"You want me to agree on the fact that I'm totally replaceable in your life?"

"But I also believe I'm replaceable in yours. There's no mystic connection here. It's timing and proximity."

"So hot, I'm swooning," she said, fanning herself.

"You hate breakfast," I said, pointing an accusing finger in her direction.

"So? How does that relate to this conversation?"

"It completely relates because I love breakfast. I firmly believe everyone should eat it, that it's the most important meal of the day. The fact that you hate it seems like a glaring character flaw. BUT, I totally accept that about you. I move on and let it go because we're different, Bellamy. I love you, but we will always, always be different. And that's okay."

She froze, staring at me, hands clenched, mouth ajar. I backtracked, wondering what new horrific thing I'd said and realized almost immediately. I swiveled forward and gripped the steering wheel, thankful for the distraction of driving. Except it turned out we were on her street. I swung into her driveway and turned off the car.

"You meant it in the friend way, right?" she asked, giving me an out. "Like, flippantly, 'You know I love you, lifelong pal, but you drive me crazy.'"

I nodded, staring resolutely ahead. "I meant it in the friend way," I agreed, my voice croaky with panic. I took a breath and made myself release the steering wheel and face her. "And also, I think I meant it in the new way, the unexpected way." I bit my lip, blinking furiously. "Too soon?"

She nodded. "But also, I think that's how I mean it, too."

I put my hands possessively on her face and drew her to me, over the console so we were nose to nose. "Not to nitpick, lovely, but you didn't actually say it."

"I'm scared."

"I was teasing. You don't have to."

"I want to. But it's kind of a big deal," she said. Her eyes were on my lips and I sort of lost the thread of the conversation because I suddenly felt so desperate to kiss her, to hold on to the moment, to her, to *us*. We had been in a camp bubble the last two weeks, in our own world, content to concentrate only on each other. But now we were home. Not only would we be physically apart for most of our time, we each had crazy big families, waiting to interfere.

As if thinking of them caused them to appear, three of her younger siblings sneaked close and surrounded the car, banging on the windows. Such was our ease with the noise and chaos that neither of us jumped or reacted in any way.

"And we're back," Bellamy said.

"No, we're still team Mulligan/Brown. You and me, secret cohorts."

"Secret? That's kind of hot, Huntley."

"That's my name. Feel free to wear it out."

She giggled, and I smiled. Bellamy had this way of laughing with all of herself. Her entire presence lit from within and burst out of her, involving not just her face, but her shoulders and even her hair. How had I never noticed before her absolute perfection? Worse, how had I chalked these adorable things up to imperfection? The hair, which used to cause me so much anxiety, was now a functioning part of our relationship. I pushed it away from her face, enjoying the corkscrew feel of it on my palm.

"There's going to be a lot of *buzz* about us when I go inside," she said nudging me while I groaned.

"No, stop it with the bee jokes."

"I'm going to have to tell them you're my ba-*bee*."

"You're a monster," I whispered, brushing her lips with mine while her siblings began to hoot and holler outside the car, pounding louder and harder on the windows.

"Yes, but I'm *your* monster," she said and my heart actually flopped, stopped, and turned over with the happiness of it.

"Don't forget," I said, still brushing my lips on hers. It was so hard to let go and drive away, even with her siblings performing percussion on my car.

"Guess I'd better return to the hive," she said, easing out of my clasp. I made a whimpering sound, totally unlike me, that made her smile. "Guess what?"

"I'm pathetic?" I guessed, my fingers still pathetically stretching toward her as she began to pull away.

She shook her head as she opened the door and mouthed the words. *I love you.*

More, I mouthed in return. She tossed me a wink and exited the car.

By the time I arrived home, my mom knew. This, I understood, was not due to Haven, who wouldn't have broken twin code, unless I was in some sort of mortal peril. That meant Bellamy's mom, Brooke, must have called. That meant the mothers had been talking. Since I had always been the good, fuss-free kid, it was strange to enter the house and see my mom staring at me with concern, flour-covered dishtowel clutched to her chest in anxiety.

"So, you and Bellamy," she said.

"Yes," I drawled, cheeks flushing in embarrassment. I'd had crushes on girls, of course, but never one that involved my mom in the conversation. She seemed content to let Haven handle the talking on that front, pumping her for information after the fact. It was a handy relay system we'd worked out. This was the first time she'd ever confronted me directly over a girl, proving how seriously she took the situation. Why, though? Because Bellamy was her best friend's daughter? Because our families were close? Or because of something else?

She heaved a sigh and twisted the towel between her fingers. "Just be careful, Huntley. Please."

"I won't hurt her, Mom," I promised, feeling slightly offended. What exactly did my mother think of me?

"It's not really her I'm worried about in this scenario," my mom said slowly.

My jaw dropped. "Mom, what's that supposed to mean? What's wrong with Bellamy?"

"Nothing," she insisted. "*Nothing.* I love Bellamy, you know that. I love all the Browns, they're our dearest friends."

"Is that what you're worried about, that I'm going to wreck your relationship with Brooke somehow?"

She shook her head, her gaze darting away. "It's…I don't know how much you know about Bellamy's…past."

"I know everything," I said. "We talked. Kind of a lot."

She gave a relieved sort of nod. "Then you'll know what she went through a few years ago."

"Yes, but it has nothing to do with us," I said, my tone vehement.

She gave me what could only be described as a pitying glance. "Oh, Huntley, honey, it has everything to do with you."

"Mom," I exclaimed, becoming overwrought with unknown emotions. I thought my mom would be so happy with this new development, believed it would be a dream come true. But now she was giving me grief about it? Because she somehow believed Bellamy was tainted by her past? She who had always taught us to bestow grace and forgiveness was now reneging on that? I felt hurt and betrayed on a number of levels. My face, as usual, probably revealed all of it.

"Please hear me out, okay? And know it's coming from a place of love, for both you and Bellamy." She took a deep breath. "I had a past before your dad. You know that. You know our teenage years were filled with some pretty wild behavior. I've tried hard to shield you kids from it, mostly because I didn't want you to repeat my mistakes. So maybe you don't realize how many scars I carry from that past."

I blinked at her, both intrigued and uncomfortable. I didn't want to hear about my mom's past or her "scars." I wanted her to merely be Mom, forever. On the other hand, a part of me realized she was offering me insight that I might soon need, specifically into Bellamy and our relationship. So I remained still and frozen, forcing myself to power through my discomfort and pay attention.

"What that man did to Bellamy was evil, a more multilayered evil than you probably realize. He not only stole things from her, he left her with scars, some she probably doesn't realize yet. She's been trying hard to overcome it, to work through a lot of those issues, and I admire that. It takes strength and grit to do that, and Bellamy has both those things. But whoever she's with, especially the first person she's with, is going to take the brunt of a lot of undeserved and unresolved issues. I guess what I'm saying is that if you want to be with her, you need to be prepared to deal with that. It's not something I've ever wanted for you. You'll notice that I've never tried to pair you two together, despite our families' long connection. That's why. Because it might take more than you're presently capable of giving, a selfless sort of maturity that might be beyond your years or understanding at this point. Not because we don't approve, because of course we do. But I'm worried. So I want you to know that if it gets to be too much, if there are things you don't understand or can't cope with, I hope you'll reach out to me or your dad or anyone else in our world you feel can help. Okay, will you promise me that? Just...don't lose Huntley in the fight to save Bellamy."

I had absolutely no idea what to say or how to respond. Camp had been the most amazing two weeks of my life. I stepped inside my house, intending that woozy feeling of love to continue, and was instead greeted with a virtual bucket of cold water in my face. By my mother, the person who I thought would be happiest over the new development. I broke eye contact and blinked at the wall, over-whelmed. It was only our good relationship and my trust in her and my dad that enabled me to tamp down my temper and respond with a neutral, "Okay." Inside, I wasn't certain I was. I sort of felt like I was seething, incensed on Bellamy's behalf, on my behalf.

Why did my mom believe Bellamy was so messed up? She seemed fine. And why did she assume I would be incapable of handling it, if so? I was *definitely* fine. I could handle anything, especially with Bellamy by my side. I resented my mom for casting a shadow on my happiness, for casting doubts on my relationship with Bellamy. But I loved and respected my parents, so the new contrast made me uncomfortable, almost sick.

My mom sighed, probably guessing more of my thoughts than I wanted her to, which was sort of her M/O in life. "Sutton, Haven, and Brian are swimming. I'm sure they'd appreciate the buffer," Mom said.

I nodded and snapped to attention, relieved to have an excuse to leave the kitchen.

"Huntley, I'm glad you're home. And I love you," Mom called after me as I headed upstairs.

"You, too," I yelled back vaguely, too upset to give her my usual bear hug.

I did give one to Haven, however, as soon as I changed into my trunks and stepped outside. Not that I had much choice in the matter, since she propelled from the pool and flung herself at me. "Huntley!"

It was such an unmitigated relief to see her I almost bawled. And even though I was the sort of guy in touch and comfortable with my emotions, it would *not* have been comfortable to cry in front of Sutton and Brian, especially Brian, Haven's best friend.

"We have so much to talk about," Haven said, giving me a squeeze.

I nodded, relief washing over me in waves because I knew everything she wanted to talk about was me and Bellamy and how it was going. Finally, I would be able to unload and process all that had happened, including the last strange conversation with Mom.

"And I'm so glad you're here," she added, giving me an extra squeeze.

"Your buffer is back," I whispered, squeezing her in return.

"Hallelujah," she said, letting me go with a laugh.

Things were always tenuous when Sutton and Brian were together. They had reached a point of agreeing to disagree, for Haven's sake. But the tension and awkwardness between them oozed to everything around them. It had been worse the last few weeks, since Brian and his girlfriend broke up. It was obvious to everyone that Sutton felt a bit insecure over his ability to keep Haven, now that Brian was free. Which was ludicrous and sort of hilarious, on a number of levels. Sutton was the most popular guy in school. Brian was, well, *not*. Sutton was going to Rhode Island with Haven, while Brian was headed to Ohio State. Plus Haven had declared—repeatedly—that Sutton was her choice and Brian was merely a friend. But still that little bit of doubt and insecurity lingered. Formerly I had made fun of Sutton for it, but now I regretted all of my joking because now I got it. Even though Bellamy and I had been fully together for the remainder of camp, I hadn't wanted to have Curt near because of her former attraction to him. How much worse must it be when the guy was her best friend since sixth grade?

"Hey, Bri," I said, tossing him a friendly wave before I picked up the football and tossed it to Sutton.

"Hey, Huntley. How was camp?"

"Awesome," I returned. That was the extent of our interaction, but it was enough. We'd always been friendly, but never friends. And that was fine because he was Haven's friend. I turned my attention to Sutton who regarded me with relieved puppy eyes.

"Dude," Sutton said, jumping to catch my bad pass. He could have been talking about the pass, as in *Dude, why did you throw that three feet over my head.* But I knew him well enough to understand his true meaning. *Dude, can you believe I still have to put up with this guy? Kill me now.*

So I laughed as I lunged to catch Sutton's bad pass back to me. We weren't usually bad at tossing the ball, but we were both clearly distracted. "Yep," I agreed.

"Bellamy Brown," Sutton said, wagging his brows as he caught the ball and tossed it back, a good pass this time, one that shot straight into my waiting grasp.

"Bellamy Brown," I agreed, my heart turning over at saying her name.

"When am I going to meet the future Mrs.?"

"Tomorrow?"

"Awesome," Sutton agreed.

That was that. We threw the ball in comfortable silence. Haven, I knew, would want every minute detail of the entire two weeks, and I would happily give them to her. But with Sutton, a few words and a lot of subtext had always been enough. Strangely, we'd always sort of gotten each other, without needing so say anything. I supposed the best friendships were like that. Or maybe not, I had no idea. Sutton was my closest friend, outside my family. Parker and I were friends, but we didn't get each other the same way. We needed more words, but Parker was a fan of talking. Sometimes I thought he spoke merely to hear himself jabber. If not for his secret—and often unused—depth, we probably wouldn't even be friends. But Parker had a good, big heart, beneath all the idiotic blather. A good thing, since Parker was my only friend sticking around next year when everyone else went away.

My little sister, Charlotte, poked her head out the door. "Huntley, you're home!" I regarded her with suspicion.

"Yes," I said, tone wary. Charlotte, Lottie to almost everyone, was only a couple of years younger than me and Haven, but we'd never been close, preferring to keep our twin bond strongly in tact. In fairness, we also weren't close to Joel, our older brother, also by two years.

"Will you take me driving tonight?" Lottie pled, hands clasped beneath her chin.

I sighed. It was the very last thing I wanted to do. I was exhausted. I wanted to talk to Haven and spend the remainder of the night on the phone with Bellamy. But I also had a responsibility to be a functioning part of the family. "A little," I agreed. "An hour, max."

"An hour would be perfection," Lottie said, now buzzing with good cheer. "You're my favorite," she added in a loudly whispered aside, causing Haven to chuck a plastic ring at her.

"That's why I don't ask you," Lottie called, disappearing from view, and also from Haven's reach.

"Dude," Sutton said, shaking his head. This one, I knew, meant, *Dude, your family is nuts. But I love them.*

"Dude," I agreed, tossing the ball toward him again.

CHAPTER 19

"You have to ease your grip. Relax. We're on a back road here, not in danger of hitting anything or anyone," I coaxed.

"I'm trying," Lottie said, teeth gritted. In a large family, we all have our assigned roles. My dad, the head of the family and also his large business, had become too busy to teach everyone to drive. It fell to the older siblings. But my older brothers were seemingly never home and Haven, as we've established, lacked the temperament for patient instruction. That meant it fell to me. And really, I didn't mind so much. Or at least I hadn't, pre-Bellamy. Then I'd had nothing better to do with my time than allow my almost sixteen-year-old sister to chauffer me around the back roads of our neighborhood. It had been kind of fun to be the big brother she needed most, the one teaching her something invaluable. Even though I was a twin, I fell solidly into the middle kid category. It was easy to get lost in a large family, especially when you did nothing to stand out. My hobbies weren't the sort that brought me adulation, not like Lottie who played the violin and sang. She'd performed in actual paying venues. Me? I had my bees and the weather. And now Bellamy.

"So you and Bellamy," Lottie mused, not risking darting me a glance.

"Yeah," I said, tone defensive. After Mom's reaction, I wasn't sure what to expect from everyone else, minus Haven.

"I love it," Lottie said.

"Yeah?" I asked, grinning now. I needed all the encouragement I could get now. "Why's that?"

"Opposites. You're all cautious and serious and Bellamy's all free-spirited and boho. Classic."

"She's more serious than she seems, once you get to know her. She wants to be a lawyer, and she's crazy smart."

"Listen to you, defending her," she said, shaking her head. "I need to see it in person, to quantify the cuteness."

"Quantify the cuteness?" I said. It was one of those girl things my sisters said that made utterly no sense to me.

"Uh, yeah. I have to know who wins the cuteness competition, you guys or Sutton and Haven. Until now, there hasn't been a contest or comparison."

"Girls are weird," I said, shaking my head.

"Yeah," Lottie agreed good naturedly. "Girls be crazy. I think that's why we have boys, to help with the fallout."

"You're going to be really popular with the feminists, when you get to college," I warned her.

"I'm not going to college," she said.

I sat up. "What? Why not? Of course you are."

"Of course I'm not. Why would I want to when I want to be a musician?"

"Because education makes you a well rounded person," I said.

"You sound like Mom and Dad in pamphlet form. I can be well rounded without dropping a hundred thousand dollars on college."

I clucked my tongue at her, disapproving. She rolled her eyes.

"I guess you have two years to change your mind," I said, confident she would.

"Only one, actually. I'm set to graduate early," she reminded me. It was a thing with homeschool. You could graduate as soon as you finished your curriculum. I could have graduated last year, too, but I held off taking my exams so I could graduate public high school with

Haven. "You should be glad I'm not going to college. Otherwise we'd be freshmen together."

It was hard to hide my grimace at that, but only because I thought of her as being a baby. "Still, I think you should go."

"Noted," she replied.

I sighed and faced forward with a muttered, "Women."

Lottie cracked up, finally removing her hand from the wheel to give my shoulder a shove. "Also noted."

"Hey, where are you going?" I asked, sitting up in alarm after a few moments of silent driving on her part.

"I thought I'd swing by the Browns' house. Stop in and say hi."

"What? No. You can't."

"Why not? It's just the Browns. We've been there a trillion times," she said.

"That was then. Now it's my girlfriend's house," I said, dabbing actual sweat from my forehead.

"Look at you, about to pass out with anxiety. Kind of adorable, if I'm being honest," she said. Then, realizing I was, in fact, about to pass out, added, "We'll blame it on me. I'll be your buffer and ease you in. It's better this way, as a casual drop in, than some staged look-at-us-we-are-together-now couple's debut. You'll see."

I chose to trust her, mostly because I didn't have any choice. We were already pulling in to the Browns' driveway. We'd been friends so long, and were the type of friends, who didn't have to give each other advance warning of visits. The Browns, as I'd already mentioned, were chaotic. Their house was always a mess. I commented on it once to my mom, in disgust, but she laughed it off. *Of course Brooke cleans. She vacuums and washes the bathrooms. But when you have ten people living in a medium size house, there's bound to be clutter and mess.*

Why isn't our house like that? I'd asked.

My mom paused before she answered. *Our house isn't medium.*

That was my first inkling that, unlike everyone else we knew, my parents were loaded. Before then I hadn't realized our house was so much bigger, nicer, decked out. It made me feel humbled, thankful, and vaguely ashamed. Bellamy's dad was an insurance agent and her mom took in sewing work on the side, occasionally selling things on Etsy. Their house was small; everyone was doubled up. Really, when I thought about it, I had no idea how they survived, especially knowing how much food our family consumed in a week. Bellamy and I both had jobs, she as a waitress and I at my dad's carwash. But my money went toward all my extras and into savings for my future. I realized, suddenly, that Bellamy's money probably went toward necessities I took for granted, like clothes and shoes. Otherwise there could be no money for so many kids. And while my parents had been putting money into a college account for each of us since we were born, I had no doubt Bellamy would have to pay for everything on her own.

"Their house is so small," I blurted. I'm sure it could be misconstrued as a rude statement, but I had no worries about Lottie being offended. Though we weren't as close as Haven and I were, she knew I wasn't mean or snobby about such things. It was just that I was seeing it anew, wondering over the struggle Bellamy must face. I'd assumed we were the same because we were both from big, homeschooling families, had previously been aggravated by her family's chaos and mass confusion. But, really, we weren't the same at all. My family enjoyed far more privilege and opportunity than hers did. I had it easy; Bellamy did not. Something I'd have to keep in mind, going forward.

"Yeah. Jacob told me they only get one present each at Christmas," Lottie said, staring at the house.

Jacob, Bellamy's fourteen-year-old little brother, was Lottie's closest friend. "Are you and Jacob, like, secretly together?" I asked.

She laughed and shook her head, nose wrinkled. "Gross, no. He's younger than me."

"Only one year."

"Still, it's not like that. Don't start pairing everybody up because you're in lurve," she warned.

I smiled and shrugged, cheeks blooming.

"Seriously, let's get you inside so I can observe this wonder for myself. Huntley in love. Wonders never cease." She shook her head.

"Why is it a wonder? I'm normal."

"If you have to tell people you're normal, you're not. Also, you're so above it all, so Zen."

"We don't believe in Zen," I reminded her.

"I wasn't using it in the literal sense. Papa don't preach. I simply meant you've always been sort of disdainful of any of the regular snares of teenage life. You didn't want Haven to go to school or date. And now look at you, doing both."

"People change, I guess," I mused. "Doesn't mean I have to like it. I really hate change, in fact."

"I know," Lottie sympathized. "But clearly it's not always bad. Right?"

"Yeah, but…"

"But what?" she prompted.

"Haven's still going away." I hated that Haven was going to Rhode Island, loathed it. I felt like a part of me was going to whither and die when she went away and, if I were being honest, I was scared. We'd never been apart before, not really. And the last year, sharing school and Sutton together, we'd been closer than ever. For the first time, we both seemed to realize how deep our bond went, how much it meant to us both, how lost we'd feel without it.

"You have six other siblings," Lottie reminded me. "I know I'm not your twin, but I'm still your sister. And I'm only two years younger."

There was a fair amount of hurt in her tone, and I hated it. I hated for any of my siblings to be sad, but especially my sisters. And this pain was kind of my fault. I knew I favored Haven, but I couldn't seem to help it. We were twins, after all.

"I know, Lottie, and I love you. You know that."

"I do. But it's different with Haven," she said, rather sadly, in my opinion.

"We've been a team since birth," I said.

"I would say this year you and I could be a team, but now there's Bellamy." She stared at the Browns' house. I stared there, too, noting the toys spilled onto the small lawn. Before, the untidiness would have annoyed me, but now I understood. With eight children in a three-bedroom house, where else was the mess supposed to go if not into the yard?

"We'll hang out," I promised her. "I have to get in all my sibling time before I go away."

"It stinks that people have to go away," she said. "Stupid Haven," she added, dashing at her eyes.

"Stupid Rhode Island," I amended, and we high fived.

Someone knocked on the door. I whirled and saw Bellamy leaning in, smiling at me. My heart stopped for a worrying amount of beats before taking off in triple time. Had I really only left her a few hours ago? It felt like four years. I rolled down the window. She leaned in, resting her forearms on the car door.

"You stalking me?" she asked.

"I'm trying so hard," I replied.

She smiled. Her glance fell to my lips, and I seriously thought maybe my heart was in trouble at that point.

"Hi, Bellamy," Lottie said, loudly and pointedly interrupting our moment with a cheerful wave.

"Hey, Lottie," Bellamy said with a friendly chuckle. "You guys coming in?"

"Well," I began, still nervous to see her mom.

"Absotutely," Lottie enthused.

"She said absotutely," I said.

"Homeschooled," Bellamy said in a stage whisper.

"All the weirdest people are," I agreed.

"I think you mean coolest," Bellamy said, tossing Lottie a wink.

"No, pretty sure he meant weirdest," Lottie agreed happily. Like most of the people in our family, she suffered no lack of self-esteem and could easily joke about her complete lack of coolness.

"Possibly," Bellamy agreed, laughing. She poked my shoulder. "Come inside, chicken."

"I'm not chicken," I said.

"He'd have to be less afraid to be a chicken," Lottie added helpfully, causing Bellamy to snort a laugh.

"You're supposed to be on my side, girlfriend," I reminded her.

She pressed her lips together, suppressing her smile. "Always and forever," she said.

"Okay, I might need to come in and use a defibrillator," I murmured, exiting the car at last.

"Whatever works for you," Bellamy said, linking her arm with mine as we dodged toys on our way toward the house. "How's the driving, Lottie?"

"Great. Huntley's a pretty good teacher," Lottie said.

"Yes, but Huntley's pretty good at everything," Bellamy said, tossing me a glance and smile that could only be described as adoring.

"What? Sorry, I was throwing up in my mouth a little," Lottie said, causing Bellamy to laugh, causing me to smile. She opened the door and stepped inside without knocking because we had that sort of relationship with the Browns and vice/versa. I was only now beginning to appreciate the closeness of our families' long histories together, now that it was applicable to my romantic life. It was nice, this shortcut I'd taken to get here. How many people get to fall in love with someone their family knows and approves of? *Does Mom approve, though?* I shoved the thought aside.

"Lottie." Bellamy's brother Jacob appeared from somewhere in the house. "You drove?"

"Yep," Lottie said, full enthusiasm.

"Awesome," Jacob agreed in the same tone. "In a few months, you'll be able to drive me places. Up top." He held up both his hands and she gave him a double high five. "Come with me, I have to show you something in my room." He turned and trooped away, Lottie trailing happily behind. I watched them go with a slight frown.

"They're not going to make out somewhere, are they?"

"No way, they're pals," Bellamy said.

"Yes, but so were we until two weeks ago," I reminded her.

"Are you certain? I'm pretty sure we've always been together," she said, slipping her arms around my waist.

"You have a good point there," I said, leaning forward to kiss her temple and surreptitiously sniff her hair.

"Did you just smell me?" she asked.

"Yep. Deal with it."

"It's fine, but I thought bees used sight?" she said, poking my stomach.

"Actually, they use scent to locate their new homes after they swarm. And since you are, in fact, my home now, I'm allowed to sniff you."

"Oh, my lands, I was trying to make fun of you, but that was so unexpectedly hot I'm actually flushed," she said, waving her hand to fan her face.

"Speaking of secret makeout locations..." I murmured, sliding my other arm around her waist.

"Huntley!"

I jumped guiltily and whirled toward the sound of Bellamy's mom, now standing at the edge of the room. "Brooke. Er..." I had always called her Brooke, but now I wondered if I shouldn't. Should I call her Mrs. Brown? I tossed Bellamy a helpless look. She responded by snorting a laugh and covering her mouth with her hand. Clearly, I was on my own here. But apparently it was fine because Brooke came forward and hugged me tightly, beaming.

"Hi, honey. It's good to see you."

"Er, you too," I said, awkwardly patting her back. Our families were pretty open and touchy, but this was the first time I ever remembered hugging Brooke.

"I'm glad you stopped by," she said. She let me go and stood back, but she was still oddly beaming. "You know you're always welcome here." Her glance darted between me and Bellamy, and I swear she got a little teary.

"Okay, Mom. Thanks, but now you're making it weird," Bellamy said.

"Right," Brooke said, trying and failing to push away her grin. "I'll go. Call if you need anything."

"Mother," Bellamy drawled, sounding pained and slightly mortified.

"I'm going, I'm going," Brooke said. She shot me one more toothy smile and disappeared back into the kitchen.

"Seriously," Bellamy whispered. "It's worse than I thought it would be. As soon as I came into the house after you dropped me off, she burst into tears and said, 'I am so happy.' I had to be like, 'Mom, we're hanging out, not getting married. You have to chill.' Good to see my pep talk worked."

I laughed and clasped her hand, letting our arms swing between us. "Come on, it's cute she's so happy. And I'm pretty relieved by it, not going to lie."

"Your mom had to have been the same," she said.

I froze. Thankfully Jacob and Lottie dashed back into the room before Bellamy could clock my expression. "Huntley, you have to come see this," Lottie declared urgently. "Jacob got an axolotl."

"What? You didn't tell me that," I launched accusingly at Bellamy. Pet news was the kind of thing the Browns and the Mulligans tracked with each other.

"It seemed like we had more important things to, um, discuss," she said, eyes dropping pointedly to my lips.

"Oh, gag," Lottie said.

"What?" Jacob said, clueless as usual.

"I'll tell you when you're older," Lottie said, snaking her arm through his.

"As long as you don't show him," I called after them.

"Aack," Lottie squealed, her noise only adding to the chaos and endless noise of Bellamy's house.

I held out my arm toward Bellamy. "Shall we see the axolotl?"

"You plan the best dates," Bellamy said, standing on her toes to kiss my cheek before threading her arm through mine.

CHAPTER 20

As I'd guessed, Haven wanted every last detail of my relationship with Bellamy. It was kind of nice, actually, to have someone so acutely interested in the details of my life, especially when it helped me categorize my own thoughts and feelings. And so important to her was our evening together that she sent Sutton home so we could hang out. I felt a little bad about that because Sutton hated to leave our house and go home. But then I reminded myself that in a few weeks he'd have her fulltime in Rhode Island and felt better. Right now was my turn; he could wait.

"It's so perfect," Haven said, tone and expression dreamy in that way girls get when they hear something romantic. "I wouldn't have put you two together, but now that it's happened, I freaking love it." She reached over to jostle my arm.

"Why wouldn't you have put us together?" I asked, somewhat defensively, a leftover from my conversation with Mom.

"Because we've had a lot of years together and you've never once shown an inkling of interest in her, not even a glance. I figured if it was going to happen, it would have by now. I mean, we've logged a lot of time with the Browns."

"Yeah, it's weird. Why do you think it suddenly changed?" I asked, pillowing my head on my hand as I faced her. We lay side by side on the basement carpet, *The Princess Bride* blaring behind us. A handful of our siblings streamed in and out of the room, occasionally sitting down to watch, but we ignored them as much as they ignored us. Haven and I had always been our bubble because, well, twins.

"Maybe seeing her in a new place allowed you to see her in a new way. You know? She wasn't Bellamy, one of the chaotic Browns. She was Bellamy, adorable girl with the plucky attitude."

"Pluckiness, that's what drew me to her," I said, uncharacteristically sarcastic.

Haven scowled. "I don't need to know the particulars of what attracted you. I've seen the girl in a swimsuit."

"Bah," I said, pressing my hand to my eyes to try and push back the mental image I definitely didn't want to have while talking to my sister. Bellamy in her hot pink one piece. Have mercy.

"Think about bees," Haven offered helpfully.

"No good, she teases me about the bees."

"As she should," she interjected.

I uncovered my eyes and shoved her. "Bees are awesome and amazing."

"Not as awesome and amazing as Huntley in love," Haven said sincerely and we shared a smile. "I'm so happy for you. It killed me to think of you all alone when I left, and now you have this amazing new relationship."

"I know," I agreed, clasping her hand and giving it a squeeze. It was the same way I was glad she had Sutton, to take care of her, to fill up all the lonely spaces. The hardest thing about being part of a pair was not being part of that pair anymore. I thought of Mom again and Haven frowned, likely reflecting my new expression.

"What?" she asked, giving my hand a worried squeeze.

"Did Mom talk to you about Bellamy?"

"Of course not. She didn't know until today, when Brooke told her. She called right before you got home and passed the gossip along."

"She's...not happy about it," I said.

Haven sat up. "What? That's not possible. It's their dream come true for one of us to get together with one of the Browns. There is no way Mom isn't ecstatic about it."

"That's how Brooke was, but Mom…she's really concerned."

She tipped her head at me. "Are you sure you weren't being overly sensitive and misconstrued things?"

It was a fair question. I did tend to be overly serious and sensitive to criticism and disappointment. "No, she said the words out loud. She's really worried about it, sort of freaked."

"But why? We've known Bellamy forever, she's the best."

"She is," I agreed, nodding. "But, no, I don't mean *but*. Something happened to Bellamy, something bad that Mom knows about. And I guess she thinks it could affect me, affect our relationship."

"Oh," Haven said, lying back down beside me. I was relieved she didn't ask me to tell her, probably because she knew I wouldn't betray Bellamy's trust that way.

"It won't," I said, because I could hear it in her tone, her new wariness and agreement with Mom.

"It's hard for me to argue, not knowing what it is, not that I want to know what it is. It's just that if it freaked Mom out, it must be pretty serious."

"It is," I said. "But I can handle it, Haven. You know I can."

Haven smiled sweetly at me. "If anyone can, it's you for sure. But it's sort of Mom's job to worry about us. Go easy on her and try not to take it personally."

"I'll try," I promised. "I guess I'm a little sad. As much as I was dreading an over the top happiness to the news of me and Bellamy, I was also kind of looking forward to it too, you know?"

"She'll get there. She probably needs a little time to adjust. You have to keep on keeping on. She'll see how happy and well adjusted you guys are and let go of the worry. Plus it's different with moms and sons, you know? You're the first one of her boys to have a girlfriend."

"Yeah, how weird is that? Seriously, what is wrong with Jonah and Joel?" Our two older brothers were in their twenties now and showed no signs of growing up or settling down.

She made a show of checking my watch. "Not enough time in the universe for that."

We cracked up, lying on the floor clutching our stomachs and laughing together as the rest of our family streamed in and out, ignoring us. Maybe one of the reasons we'd always glommed on to each other was that easy ability to get lost in the shuffle. I thought of my earlier conversation with Lottie and vowed to spend more time with her this year. But not now, not when I had a few more weeks with Haven.

"Seriously, though, Huntley. Do not mention Mom's disapproval to Bellamy. Not ever."

I sobered at her suddenly intense warning. "Why not? I kind of tell her everything now."

She shook her head slowly. "Don't tell her this, I mean it. You'll devastate her. It's not the sort of thing a girl gets over, to hear that her future mother in law disapproves of her for some perceived flaw."

I flinched. "We're not engaged."

She stared at me.

I grinned. "Yet."

She beamed. "Swear it on your life. Don't tell."

"I won't tell," I promised, linking our pinkies together. "So, tomorrow. We have to think of something fun and fantastic to do. It's technically only my second date with Bellamy. I need to make a good impression. And you have to be extra nice to her. She's super nervous about meeting you."

"Meeting me?" Haven asked, clutching her stomach as she burst into a new round of giggles. "She met me when she was three days old."

That part was true. We had pictures of us as one year olds holding a newborn Bellamy, looking terrified and traumatized by the little pink bundle in our arms.

"You know what I mean. Everything is different now. I was really freaked out to see Brooke."

"Everything might be different for you guys, but nothing is different for me. I already regarded Bellamy as a sister from another mother. It's still the same, only now I'll be watching obsessively for signs of romance between you. Kind of exciting." For emphasis, she clapped her hands together.

"Awesome," I said dryly.

"We could always invite Parker along as an extra. That would definitely diffuse any tension."

That was true, it was impossible to be tense with Parker nearby. I loved him, but the boy never stopped talking. "Nah, that might make Bellamy more nervous."

"Right," Haven said, reading the truth behind my words. "And it's not at all because you don't want Bellamy exposed to Parker and his charm or cuteness."

"Bellamy and I are solid," I declared. Then, "Oh, shut up. He's an insane flirt, and you know it. I might actually kill him, if he spent the whole night hitting on her."

"Which he totally would," Haven agreed. "But Bellamy wouldn't take the bait. Anyone with half a brain can see through Parker's nonsense in a nanosecond, and Bellamy's fairly brilliant."

"She really is," I agreed, tone ridiculously dreamy. Then, "Oh, shut up. Don't be smug. I had to listen to you rattle on about Sutton for *months*."

"What are you talking about? I still rattle on about him."

"True story," I said. "But I've learned how to tune you out."

"Teach me how. I have a feeling I'm going to need it."

"It's going to be hard to hear from Rhode Island," I said and instantly felt bad when her expression turned wounded. "Which I totally support," I added belatedly.

"You're a terrible liar, Huntley Mulligan. But you're the best brother in the world, so I'll allow it." She scooted closer and rested her head on my shoulder. I tipped my head, resting it on hers.

Her phone beeped with a text from Sutton. I could tell by the tone and the way she tensed. "Ignore it," I warned. "Twin time."

My phone beeped with a text from Bellamy. I tensed and forced my hand away from my pocket.

"That Bellamy?" Haven asked.

"Yep," I answered.

We lay in silence a few more minutes, staring desolately at the ceiling.

"Agree twin time is over for the night?" Haven asked.

"Yep," I said, and we both lunged for our phones.

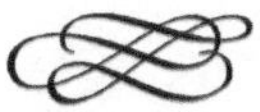

CHAPTER 21

"I'm not sure I've ever been this nervous," Bellamy said and, to be honest, she looked as scared as she said. It was odd because I didn't think of her that way. Bellamy was one of those people who seemed comfortable with herself, comfortable in every situation. The fact that it was Haven and Sutton making her feel this way made me feel a mixture of terrible and happy. Terrible because she felt bad, happy because it was so important to her to make a good impression on my best friends.

I parked in our driveway after picking her up at her house, reached across the console, and pulled her into my lap.

"Um, if anyone looks outside, they'll see us," she warned, still sounding anxious.

"No one can see this spot from the house. I checked." I wagged my brows at her.

"The advantage to living in a mansion," she murmured in my ear, kissing my lobe. Even though what she was doing was heavenly, I tensed. "What?" she said, easing back.

"Does it bother you, our house?" I asked. I had never given the disparity between our families much thought before, focusing instead on all the similarities—mass amount of kids, homeschooled, strict parents. But now the unfair weight of our family's financial status made me feel awkward and vaguely guilty.

Bellamy, being Bellamy, laughed, a tinkling sound of deep amusement. "Yes, Huntley. I'm completely offended by your massive and beautiful house, filled with wonderful people and fun things I've played with for seventeen years. Ick, let me go so I can stalk away and show you my revulsion."

"Wouldn't you be sad, if I did?" I asked, tightening my grip on her waist.

"Let me show you how much," she said. Cupping my face in her hands, she kissed me properly, our first real kiss since we left camp. Some sound startled us apart, which was good because we were starting to lose our heads, there in the driveway of my parents' house.

"So, yeah, to reiterate, kissing works well," Bellamy said. She rested her forehead on mine, eyes closed, and took a deep and shaky breath.

"I'm not convinced. Can we try again?" I asked.

She laughed and pushed away from me, sliding back to her side of the car. "Do I look as disheveled as I feel?" She touched her swollen lips self-consciously.

"You look beautiful," I assured her, reaching out to touch her cheek. "So, so insanely beautiful it's not fair to other girls."

She blinked at me, eyes bright. "Do you really think I'm beautiful? Like, you're not saying that to be nice and a good boyfriend?"

"I think you're the most beautiful girl in the entire world, and I know you know me better than to think I'm lying for the sake of anything," I said, resting my head on the chair behind me as I tried to take her in. She had made extra effort to look good tonight, doing something to try and tame her flyaway hair so she could leave it down. Despite having multiple sisters, I had no idea about makeup, but Bellamy had done something there, too, something that made her face shimmery and sparkly, her lashes extra long and thick. And even though I appreciated the extra steps, I found her equally as beautiful without makeup, the way she'd been on those early morning bus trips and when she woke up in my room the day she slept over. Maybe other girls were more objectively beautiful, but none of them were mine; that made it better somehow, more special, as if her prettiness was just for me.

"You're so good at this," she whispered. "So, so good, Huntley. How did you get so perfect?"

"I'm not," I assured her. "You know I'm not."

"But you are, you always have been, even before you were mine."

Far from making her happy, the thought seemed to make her sad. Now her pretty eyes were sparkling with tears. "Bellamy, hey. What's this about?"

She shook her head.

"Talk to me," I pled, squeezing her shoulder. She swallowed hard and took a shaky breath.

"I feel so inadequate, so completely messed up sometimes. So broken." She tapped her heart. "Inside."

I put my arms around her and pulled her against my chest, cradling her in a gentle hug. "I love you. I think you're amazing."

She gave a watery little laugh. "Why, exactly? What is it about this pathetic moment that speaks to you?"

"It's not only this moment, it's all the moments. You're smart and fun and funny, competitive and quirky and, did I mention, totally beautiful." I kissed the top of her head, pausing to inhale.

"Creepy sniffer," she said, but she slid her arms around me and squeezed tightly. "I really love you, Huntley. Right now I mean that in the friend way, but in some ways that's even bigger and more important to me." She pulled back a little. "I don't trust many people outside my family. I don't have a lot of friends who don't share my DNA. Mostly you and your family. And you mean so much to me. The fact that I can trust you and have fun with you, it's like icing on a cake I received by accident."

"Same. All of it," I said. I wanted to kiss her again, but it didn't seem like the time. I settled for kissing her cheek instead.

She groaned and rested her head on my shoulder. "You're the absolute sweetest ever."

"I really am," I agreed, which made her laugh, which made me smile. "You ready to get this date on the road?"

"Yes?"

"Was that a question?"

"No?"

"Come on, chicken." I gave her another squeeze and let her go. "Let's go let Haven fawn over you a while as Sutton and I commiserate."

"I'm anxious to see them together," she said, perking up. "Haven's so intimidating. It's hard to imagine her being with anyone."

"She's found her match, for certain. Fair warning: they are both competitive. Don't let them drag you into a game. You'll lose. Badly."

She pursed her lips. "You think so?"

"Oh, geez. I forgot you're also like them. The three of you are going to obliterate me tonight."

"I'll protect you," she said, sliding her arm around my waist and giving me a squeeze.

Haven opened the door and rested her hand on her hip. "Huntley, get in here and referee. Sutton is cheating at the burrito tossing game and I might stab him. Oh, hey, Bellamy."

Bellamy froze and regarded me with an upward tilt of her head. "Or maybe we'll stick together and keep each other safe," she amended.

"I really do love you," I said, kissing the top of her head.

"Same," she agreed, giving my waist a squeeze. Together, we walked into the house. Sutton was the first person we saw. He wore my youngest sister Margaret like a cape, and he was clearly cheating at the burrito game, using Margaret to deflect and toss, despite the fact that it wasn't their turn.

"You see what I'm dealing with," Haven said, motioning to him in disgust. To me the sight was adorable. Sutton fit seamlessly into our family; we had all accepted him as one of us, and I loved that he felt comfortable enough to let down his guard. (And brave enough to cheat when Haven was in competitive grizzly mode, something I didn't have the nerve to do, for certain.) I glanced at Bellamy, expecting her to share my joy, and found her scowling at Sutton instead.

"You," she said, crossing her arms over her chest.

"Uh-oh," he said, coming to a stand still as Margaret slid limply off his back.

"You two know each other?" I said, tone wary.

"Please don't tell me you made out," Haven said, tense voice matching mine.

"No," Bellamy said. "I didn't recognize you from your picture because I was looking at Haven. I do now."

"Um, how?" I asked.

"He came into the restaurant where I waitress with these two girls," Bellamy began.

"Mean One and Mean Two," Haven interjected.

"Exactly," Bellamy nodded at her, relieved to have an ally. Meanwhile Sutton and I traded panicked glances because those girls, Reagan and Addison, were our friends from school. And, okay, sometimes they could be not so nice, especially to other girls.

"Okay, I know that was a bad day," Sutton began, eyes darting in panic. Reagan and Addison were sore points with Haven, too. "But can I say for the record that it was right after Haven broke up with me. I was in a pretty bad place and acting out. And I did leave you a tip."

"Under an upside down glass of water," Bellamy said, unrelenting in her ire.

Sutton made it worse by snickering and tossing me a smile. "Some of my finest work."

"Dude, no," I said, shaking my head.

He sobered and faced Bellamy, palms out in meek surrender. "I was admittedly a jerk, and I'm sorry. But I've totally reformed, I swear." He glanced at Haven for encouragement.

"It's true, he has, bad taste in friends notwithstanding," she agreed.

"Okay, clean slate," Bellamy said, reaching out to shake Sutton's hand with a smile. "As long as I never have to see those girls again."

Haven made a sound like a choking crow and darted an amused glance to me. "Um," she drawled while I frantically shook my head. Bellamy noted the motion and focused her laser glare on me.

"Don't tell me you're friends with those girls," she said.

"Um," I began. I suddenly understood the urge to tug my collar because it felt like I was choking.

Her hands returned to her hips. "Don't tell me you made out with them."

"Um," I repeated, and now Haven joined the outrage, whirling so her ire was directed at me. I could practically feel Sutton sag with relief at not being in her headlights.

"What? You made out with them?"

"In Huntley's defense, pretty much everyone in our group has made out with Addison and Reagan," Sutton said, then had immediate regrets when Haven's ire returned to him. "I meant shut up, Sutton, okay. Hey, Babe, I love you. You look so pretty." He drew Haven close and kissed her cheek.

"One night they talked me into playing spin the bottle with them," I said. "I realized immediately it was a weird mistake, and it never happened again."

"Huh," Bellamy said. She squinted at me. I could tell she was trying to decide how mad at me she was allowed to be. I pressed my advantage by taking a step forward.

"We weren't together then. If we had been, obviously I wouldn't have done it. And it's not like it is with you, not at all." I eased closer and nuzzled her neck.

"Oh, wow, Huntley has game," Sutton muttered, watching us.

"More than you, apparently," Haven said, maintaining her irritation with him.

"Really?" he asked, leaning closer to nuzzle *her* neck, which caused her to giggle and melt into him.

"Well, it's debatable," she admitted.

"While we're all made up, can we please go? I'm starving," I said, easing my arm around Bellamy's waist.

"I would complain about boys and their stomachs, but I'm starving too," Haven agreed. "Let's go before Mom realizes our plan to stuff ourselves with junk food and tries to feed us something healthy."

"I have rye bread in the oven," Mom called, making us realize she'd been eavesdropping on us the whole time. I flushed, remembering my admitted makeout session with Reagan and Addison, whom my mom definitely did not like. The only reason I'd been allowed to hang out with them or have them over was because I assured my mom our relationship was strictly platonic, which it was. Just because they're hot and my hormones got the better of me one night didn't mean I wanted to be with either of them in the long run. They were definitely the kind of girls who were fun for a minute but not a lifetime. Not like Bellamy, who would be a fun girlfriend and a good mom to her someday children.

"What?" she asked, making me realize I was staring at her in startled silence while I had these thoughts. I was only eighteen. Should I be thinking of the mother of my future children? Then again, if not now, when? After it was already too late and I was married to someone?

"Nothing," I said, but I picked up her hand and kissed it. She flushed and my heart squeezed. I loved, loved, *loved* this girl. The unexpected joy of that was something I might never get used to, made even better by the fact that she loved me in return. "I just like you a lot."

"Same," she agreed, giving my hand a squeeze.

It was hard to imagine everything not being as amazing as it felt right now, that we might have a someday when hard things happened, when we hurt each other or broke each other's hearts. If I'd realized how soon someday would appear, I think I would have stood there a while longer, staring at her in deep appreciation of our bliss.

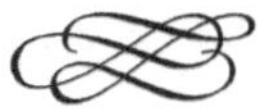

CHAPTER 22

The double date was everything I could have wanted it to be. Bellamy slid seamlessly into our group, making us a pleasant foursome instead of leaving me as the third wheel like usual. She and Haven had always been the sort of friends who could pick up and set down their friendship, not staying in contact, but resuming where they left off as soon as they were together again. It was the same tonight. They chatted endlessly about anything and everything. Usually I left them to it, but tonight I hung on their conversations, eavesdropping to gain some new or unknown insight into Bellamy.

"I haven't heard you mention the weather once since you returned from camp," Sutton noted, watching me with a grin as I watched Bellamy.

"I decided to go into medicine," I informed him, mostly to wipe the smug amusement off his face, which I succeeded in doing.

He sat up. "No way. Really?"

I nodded. "Bellamy helped me figure some stuff out. Medicine for a career, weather for a hobby."

"And bees," Bellamy added with a poke, making me realize I wasn't the only one eavesdropping tonight.

"Always bees." I returned her poke. "They're my favorite."

"They've definitely grown on me," she said.

"You should have that looked at," I said, and Sutton groaned.

"Oh, man, you found someone who employs bee humor with you. It's kismet."

"I know, right?" Bellamy said, sitting forward in earnest excitement. "This one doesn't believe in serendipity."

"A family trait," Sutton said, tossing Haven a sullen glance.

"What? Haven, you don't believe, either?" Bellamy said.

Haven shrugged. "I'm more a proximity sort of girl," she said, and I snickered.

"Dead, heartless family," Bellamy said, and Sutton high fived her.

"That's what I've been saying. I mean, seriously, we're actual star-crossed lovers, our school's epitome of Romeo and Juliet, and Haven insists it was all happenstance." Sutton sat back and rolled his eyes.

Haven and I exchanged glances and shrugs. "We Mulligans are pragmatic," Haven said.

"Pragmatic. That's so hot," Sutton said, fanning himself.

"We don't have to be the same. We can agree to disagree," I added helpfully.

"Yes, except your disagreement means you see nothing special about us," Bellamy said, motioning between herself and Sutton. "We could be anyone sitting here, not a one in a billion match."

"Our families are best friends," I said, spreading my hands wide in frustration. "The chances of one of us falling for the other are astronomical, with all the time we've logged together."

"But none of them did, none of them but us. And why is that? Maybe because we're meant to be. Maybe that's why our moms became friends in the first place, in order to give us a chance to meet," Bellamy said.

Sutton applauded her. "Exactly, Bellamy. Exactly. Maybe that's why my last church broke apart, so my parents would go to Haven's church, giving me and Huntley the chance to meet and become friends, giving Haven and I the chance to fall in love."

Haven and I looked at each other and traded shrugs. "You guys are crazy," Haven said.

"You guys are soulless," Bellamy returned. She and Sutton high fived. I knew we were all joking, mostly, but I didn't like Bellamy and Sutton being united on a team against us.

"Maybe someday we'll change our minds," I inserted.

"But I doubt it," Haven added. She was probably right. She and Sutton had been together on and off for over a year now. If it hadn't happened for them, it probably wouldn't happen for Bellamy and me. I didn't see myself morphing suddenly into a diehard romantic.

"Hopeless," Sutton said, gathering Haven close and giving her a squeeze. "But I love you anyway."

Bellamy and I traded glances. "Do you love me anyway?" I whispered, only half joking. How upset was she, really, over my pragmatic approach to our relationship?

She nodded, eased closer, and rested her head on my shoulder. That didn't exactly give me the answer I was looking for, but it gave me some reassurance. I kissed the top of her head and patted her knee. She gave a contented little sigh and sort of sagged into me. I liked that sag. It seemed somehow like an admission of trust. I wanted Bellamy's trust; I wanted all of Bellamy.

After supper we went dancing at some place Sutton and Haven frequented. "This reminds me of prom," Bellamy said as we swayed slowly on the floor. When we first arrived we'd line danced, which was fun. But this was even better, lost in our own little world as we now were.

"Not me. Prom wasn't like this at all," I said. I went with Parker, Reagan, and Addison. By then I had realized that Reagan and Addison were predatory and competitive with each other over their predation. They had decided ahead of time to divide and conquer Parker and me. Fortunately for both of us, Parker and I realized ahead of time that we were the game and they were the hunters and weren't willing to play along. Things became sort of awkward when we both refused their advances, insisting instead to keep things platonic. The whole thing was a bit of a fiasco, made better only when Parker and I finally ditched them and spent the rest of the night at our house with Haven and Sutton. "I should have asked you."

"How would that have gone, I wonder," she said, tipping her head at me in amusement that felt familiar. "Seeing as how our former pre-camp M/O was for me to tease you and you to find me annoying."

"You still tease me," I said.

"And do you still find me annoying?" she asked.

She was so adorable, I couldn't stand it. "Extremely," I said, leaning down to touch my nose to hers.

"Shucks for me," she said, standing on her toes to touch her lips to mine.

"I like a girl who can pull off 'shucks' in real life," I said.

"Homeschool, baby," she said, smiling.

"That's right, you are my homeschool baby," I said.

"Oh, swoony swoon," she said, beaming.

We finished the night back at our house. Parker was waiting on us when we arrived. Like Sutton, he'd started claiming our family for his own, showing up uninvited to hang out, whether or not we were home. Normally I didn't mind, but I was a tiny bit possessive of my time with Bellamy now, and a tiny bit apprehensive about Parker's presence. Besides Sutton, he'd been the most popular guy at our school.

He had been sitting beside Lottie as she played her guitar on the porch. He stood at our approach, squinting at Bellamy. "Um, hello," he said.

"Hello," she responded. "Are you a long lost Mulligan cousin?" She'd met some of our extended family, but not all.

"Sure," Parker said, shrugging. When she glanced at Lottie, remarking on her guitar, Parker caught my attention and mouthed, *So hot.*

I know, I mouthed in return.

"Who are you?" Parker asked her.

"Bellamy," she replied, extending her hand.

He took it, holding it a few beats too long. "Beautiful friend."

"What?" I said. Maybe I snapped it because Parker's eyes flew to me in question.

"It's what her name means in French, beautiful friend. Dude, I told you to take French instead of Latin," Parker replied.

Now Bellamy beamed at me. "You took Latin last year?"

"Medicine, baby," I replied, snatching her free hand and giving it a kiss.

"Law, baby," she replied, tugging my hand close to kiss it.

"Fifth wheel, baby," Parker said, and everybody laughed.

"What's your name?" Bellamy asked him.

"I'm Parker," he said. I was glad to hear he'd dropped the flirty undertone, having discerned Bellamy was mine, mine, mine.

"Oh, you're the guy who took Huntley's homecoming date," she said.

Far from being offended, Parker beamed. "You've heard of me?"

She laughed. "You're notorious, fifth wheel."

"Take comfort, Parker. Fifth wheel campers are the best," Haven said, linking her arm companionably with his.

"You're so odd, Mulligan. If you hadn't turned out to be shockingly hot beneath all the nerd, I'd totally tell Sutton to dump you," Parker said, squeezing her neck affectionately.

"I would totally listen," Sutton said dryly, a lie.

"Can we start this whole night over? Nothing is going my way," Parker complained.

"For once, you mean," Haven said. "You forgot to add that part."

He huffed and stamped his foot, causing Haven to laugh and Sutton to smile. Bellamy and I exchanged smiles.

"Come watch a movie with us," Haven suggested, tugging him toward the door. "You can be our chaperone so my parents won't freak out."

"Lottie, come with so I'll have someone to talk to when they all start making out," Parker said, holding out his hand to her.

"Wow, what an amazing offer," Lottie said, but she set her guitar aside and allowed Parker to clasp her hand.

"I've never been in the Mulligan basement with the intent to makeout before," Bellamy whispered. "Feels kind of weird."

"You get used to it pretty quickly," Sutton added.

"You really do," Lottie agreed. Everyone froze and stared at her. "What? I was totally joking, sheesh."

"Didn't have to be a joke," Parker said, and everyone stopped to stare at him. "Also joking, man. You Mulligans and your emphasis on personal responsibility really harsh my buzz sometimes."

"Word," Lottie agreed and Haven and Sutton separated them, inserting themselves between the only non-couple in the room.

CHAPTER 23

The next day Bellamy came over to swim. Sutton and Haven were immersed in some kind of diving competition, leaving me and Bellamy free to focus on each other. Currently she floated on a raft while I held on to the edge, trying once again not to ogle her in her hot pink swimsuit. I was not a neon person, but it definitely worked for her, bringing out the tan undertones of her skin, the brown of her hair and eyes.

"We need to talk," I said.

"That sounds ominous," she said, regarding me through her shades.

"As if I would bring up anything ominous," I said.

"Good point. What do we need to talk about, boyfriend?"

The word jolted me. In a shockingly short amount of time, this girl had gone from cute Bellamy Brown to gorgeous Bellamy, girlfriend. Sometimes my mind still had trouble making the leap, along with my galloping heart and hormones. "Hello," Bellamy said, stroking her finger along the back of my hand.

"That doesn't help with the thinking," I said, stilted and awkward.

She laughed. "At least I have an effect on you."

"Uh, yeah. That is not in doubt in any way," I said, trying to yank my mind into focus instead of thinking how much I wanted to kiss her at that moment. At every moment. *Want, want, want, need, need, need.* Those seemed to be my only coherent thoughts when I was with her lately. So much for being a gentleman. I was apparently turning into every moronic guy I'd ever looked down on. I shook my head, accidentally spraying her with droplets from my wet hair. *Focus, Huntley.* On what, though? I honestly couldn't remember.

"You said we need to talk," she prompted, looking amused by my idiocy.

"Right, talk. Yes. About next year."

"What about it?" she asked.

"Which college are we going to go to?"

She sat up slightly, jostling the raft. I held it steady so she wouldn't fall off. "You want to go to college together?"

"Don't you?" I said.

"I hadn't actually thought that far ahead," she said.

"How far ahead have you thought?" I asked. Because I was thinking about forever. Wasn't she?

"I mean, I've thought ahead, but I guess I sort of skipped over the practicality of college, thinking we'd be together wherever we end up because, you know," she shrugged, "meant to be and all. But I forgot to take into account that you need proximity." She was clearly teasing me, as usual. As if to magnify that fact, she winked and touched my cheek with her finger.

"I don't *need* proximity. I *want* proximity."

"You are so good at boyfriending," she said, nearly upending the raft again as she leaned close to kiss me.

"Yeah? Why don't you get down off that raft and prove it," I suggested.

She glanced around for Haven and Sutton, who were mostly submerged at this point, and then slid off the raft into my arms.

"It's cold," she complained.

"Let me warm you," I suggested. I snagged her around the waist and pressed her against me, holding her aloft in water that was over her head.

"I'm dependent on you for life now," she said.

"Finally," I said and smiled when she laughed.

"So, college," she began.

"College," I agreed, my heart rate picking up. We were about to set on a momentous path toward our future, so of course my mother picked that time to open the back door and step outside.

"Blah," Bellamy shrieked and tried to jump away from me. Of course she couldn't because the water was a foot over her head. So she hovered somewhere half a foot away, treading water.

"Oh, hi, Bellamy," my mother said.

"Hi, Marla," Bellamy squeaked.

Mom squinted toward the end of the pool. "The granola I made earlier has cooled, and the yogurt is ready. When Haven and Sutton emerge, let them know, okay?"

"Okay," Bellamy said.

"Well, good to see you," Mom said.

"Mm, hmm," Bellamy replied.

Mom went inside. I tried to anchor Bellamy to me, but she resisted. "You know I'm all that's keeping you afloat here, right, Short-ie?" I said.

She faced me with big, luminous eyes. "Your mom hates me."

"What? Of course she doesn't. You know my mom loves you," I said.

She shook her head. "She loved me as her best friend's daughter. As her son's girlfriend, she loathes me."

"She does not loathe you," I said, inwardly squirming. My mom didn't loathe her, I knew. That part was true. But my mind flashed to what Haven had said about never letting her know Mom's true feelings. "How could you possibly think that from that fifteen second interaction?"

She ignored my words and stared at me, possibly reading my soul. "She doesn't like us together. Tell me I'm wrong."

"I..." My eyes focused somewhere over her shoulder. Now would be a good time for Sutton and Haven to emerge with a distraction, so of course they didn't. "She has some concerns, that's all."

"Why?" Bellamy breathed.

Oh, no. She was going to make me say it. I looked at her with all the misery I felt, wishing I could disappear. "Because of your past, of what happened to you."

She paled. "You told her?"

"No, absolutely no. I would never. I didn't even tell Haven. It was probably your mom. You know how they share parenting stuff."

She used her free hand to swipe at her overflowing eyes. "She had no right to tell her that."

"I agree with you," I said.

She stared toward the horizon, tears leaking slowly down her face. My heart wrenched at her misery. "Bellamy, please, please don't be upset."

"Upset? Why would I be upset that my boyfriend's mom thinks I'm a harlot?"

"That is not what she thinks, not at all. She just…" I trailed away, not wanting her to know what my mom actually said, that she was worried I wouldn't be able to handle the fallout from Bellamy's trauma. "Haven thinks it's a mother/son thing, that Mom is freaking out because you're my first girlfriend. It's a good theory. Joel and Jonah are hopeless, as we know. That means all the pressure's on me to break the mold." I gave her a squeeze. "Please. You know she loves you. You *know* that. She just needs some time to adjust. Please don't freak out."

She nodded and swiped at her eyes, pasting on an unconvincing smile.

"Please," I whispered, giving her a squeeze. "Please let this go. I love you, and I wouldn't change a thing about you, about us. Doesn't that count for anything?"

She nodded and swiped at her eyes again. "It's just…I was a victim in that whole scenario, and I'm still stigmatized from it. Unfair, you know?"

"I do," I said. I felt the unfairness along with her. She gave me a sad smile and rested her head on my shoulder. I rubbed a little circle on her back. "I think you're doing great."

"That's because you can't see inside my head," she whispered, then slid both arms around me and gave me a tight hug that made me forget everything but her and this moment.

CHAPTER 24

The thing with my mom lingered heavily between us like a shroud. Bellamy didn't come out and say it, but I could tell. For one thing, she was no longer eager to hang out at my house. I had to coax her over, with promises of Haven and Sutton and even Parker and Lottie as buffers between her and my parents.

And then, nine days after the pool conversation, it was time to take Haven to college.

"I halfway wish I could go with you, for moral support," Bellamy said. "But I also know you need this time, just the two of you."

"The three of us," I amended. I didn't resent Sutton's place in Haven's life, usually, but I sort of had the dream of the two of us driving to college together, getting in a little twin time before I had to let her go. Instead it was the three of us in Sutton's car, my parents driving on their own in front of us. We would all drop Sutton at his school before taking Haven to hers. Sutton's dad still didn't have his license after his DUI, and his mom felt like she couldn't drive the entire way. Plus he didn't really have the sort of relationship with his parents we had with ours. Or even he had with ours. If not for us, he would likely be seeing himself off. When I thought of it that way, it was a lot easier to nip my resentment before it could take hold.

And, I had to admit, it was fun, this first taste of independence and adventure. It almost made me regret not going away myself this year. If not for Bellamy, I would probably be feeling a lot of angst at being left behind. As it was, I could be glad she and I would begin our freshman year at the same time, wherever we decided to end up. Since the conversation in the pool, we hadn't had a chance to circle back.

We still need to talk about college, I texted her.

I still need to graduate high school, she replied, along with a gif of a creepy old man.

This trip is making me impatient for our future, I returned.

our future she sent back, along with a bunch of heart emojis.

You're purposely ignoring my attempts to talk about college, I accused.

I purposely have no idea about college. You choose somewhere good and I'll apply, she said.

You have to have input, I said.

Nope. I trust you, and I'm frozen at the thought. Would seriously love you to choose.

We could go anywhere, I said, feeling overwhelmed. North, south, east, west, cold weather, hot weather. How was I supposed to choose a locale?

Now you see why I've been frozen. Seriously, choose whatever and I'll get an app.

I was suddenly and ridiculously glad we'd be going together. The thought of going somewhere on my own was overwhelming, lonely and, if I'm being honest, kind of terrifying. *I miss you. Eight hours seems far.*

It IS far, she agreed. *But have fun anyway. Take a picture of their rooms for me so I can get the full experience. PS. Bet you cry when saying goodbye.*

I wouldn't take that bet, I told her. I already felt emotional.

You're the cutest, and I love you the most. XOXO.

Same, I sent back, smiling stupidly at my phone as I reread her texts.

"Oh, man, is that how we look?" Sutton asked Haven.

"You, maybe," she said.

"Uh, no, both," I inserted.

"Yeah, he's pretty irresistible," Haven said, leaning over to rest her head on Sutton's shoulder.

"Back at you, girl," Sutton replied, squeezing her knee.

Haven sighed. "A whole week until I see you again."

Sutton frowned through the windshield, remaining silent.

To me it was amazing they were both going to be so close, their colleges only twenty five minutes apart. To them a week seemed like a lifetime. I got that now, feeling ridiculously adrift the farther we drove from Bellamy. What was it about love that made you want to physically bind yourself to that person at all times?

"A week of new people and new experiences, though," Haven added, as though to cheer herself.

"I hate new people and new experiences," Sutton said, morose. "I only like Mulligans now."

Haven looked at him all dreamy and besotted. "You can be a hermit and I'll make friends, and then my friends can become your friends."

"A plan that will probably work well the remainder of our lives," he said, squeezing her knee again.

She laughed and I smiled, watching them. It was inconceivable to me now that they would ever break up. They were too much a part of each other, too much a part of *me. They're meant to be.* I could hear it in Bellamy's voice and tried to shrug it away. They'd spent a lot of time with each other, enough to fall in love and entwine their lives with each other, along with the rest of our family. Sutton was practically one of us now, a fact proved true when my parents went to the store and loaded his mini fridge with milk, cheese sticks, fruit, and yogurt before my mom unloaded an entire case of homemade healthy treats she'd made for him.

"Remember to eat lots of fruits and veggies," she told him, hugging him in a tight Mom hold as we stood in his new room, saying goodbye.

"There's going to be lots of temptation," my dad said when it was his turn for a hug. "Call one of us or your sponsor."

Sutton was an alcoholic, six months sober now. I wondered how hard it would be to be a college freshman at a state school. Already the smell of beer and vomit permeated his hallways. But, I reasoned as Sutton let go of my dad and latched on to Haven, he'd likely be spending all his weekends with her.

I took my own turn hugging Sutton, feeling embarrassed when I sniffled. But then we pulled apart and Sutton dashed at his own eyes. "Love you, man," he said, surprising me.

"Love you, too," I said, giving him a bro-type fist bump that restored us both to our comfort zones.

"We love you, honey," my mom said, giving him one more hug. "We're here, if you need anything. No matter what."

Sutton nodded and dashed at his eyes again. I stood back and observed, feeling that little spark of bitterness again. Of course I wanted my family to love Sutton, my best friend and Haven's boyfriend. But why was it so easy with him and so hard with Bellamy, girl we'd known forever? It wasn't fair; it wasn't fair at all.

We all stepped out of the room so Haven and Sutton could say their goodbyes in private. I leaned on the wall as my mom leaned on my dad. "Is he going to be okay?" she whispered.

"We have to trust that he'll be fine," my dad said, rubbing her back.

"Why does everything have to be so hard," my mom murmured, which was a surprise to me. My mom was one of those people always striving, always moving forward, not given to complaining much. To hear her lament how hard everything was was disconcerting on a number of levels.

"It's going to be okay, honey," my dad said.

I looked away, pretending not to listen, but I couldn't help it. And the tone of the conversation was familiar to me because it was like my conversations with Bellamy. She was uncertain and anxious, I was calm and reassuring. Should I be heartened that I was like my dad or distressed that Bellamy was like my mom? They say guys always marry their moms, but gross. No one wants to think about it that way.

Haven emerged from Sutton's room dry eyed but made a beeline for me, pressing her face to my chest. "Why is this so hard? I'm only going to be a half hour away. I'll see him this weekend."

"Because it's new and different," I said, hugging her tightly. "I've been telling you for years those things are no good. Staying exactly the same, that's where it's at."

She laughed, which was my intended effect, as she pulled away and swiped her teary eyes. I kissed her forehead and rested my arm on her shoulders, leading her back to the car. She sighed, and I knew she was gearing herself up for the next goodbye, the one that would include me.

For that one, we both cried, and not a little. It wasn't that I was leaving my sister and lifelong best friend in Rhode Island, it was more that this was the first step away from each other in what would probably be a lifetime of steps away from each other. Jobs, marriages, children, relocations. For the rest of our lives, we would spend them apart, probably living in different cities, in different circumstances. Haven's job would likely take her to New York City. Sutton would follow because he'd already committed to do so. I would either return to our hometown or find somewhere else, but it wouldn't be New York. That wasn't my scene.

Never again would we belong only to each other and our parents. It was a rather soul crushing realization. Some people couldn't wait to grow up, move away, get married, start the next chapter in their lives. I wanted to stay exactly as it was, with the new addition of Bellamy. If I had my druthers, I'm move her in with us, and Sutton, too. We'd all live at home together and continue to spend all of our time with each other, the fearsome foursome. Instead Haven and Sutton would make new friends, have new adventures. And what of Bellamy and I?

Do you think we should get married before we go to college?

Of course I realized the text was a mistake as soon as I sent it. Confirmation of that came when Bellamy sent me a picture of her face, eyes wide with a scary amount of panic and the caption. *I am not your security blanket, Huntley Mulligan.*

Sigh. I know. I'm sorry. This is hard. I sent it from emotion, not thought. Of course that's not what I think we should do, and I'm happy with where we are. Please forget the crazy.

It's OK. I love the crazy, too; I love it all.

Back at you, I said.

That's only because you haven't seen how deep my crazy goes. Unknowable depths.

Um, I basically just proposed to you and we've been dating a month, I reminded her. *Pretty sure I win this round.*

I'll let you have this one, she conceded. *But only because you're so cute.*

We drove away from Haven's college campus, and I felt sad. But as I stared at my phone and ran my finger over Bellamy's picture, I couldn't help but think this year had definite possibility to be the best one ever.

CHAPTER 25

Lottie made me cookies when I got home. It was sweet how hard she was trying to fill the Haven void. In return, I took her driving an extra long time.

I smell like fried food. Bellamy had started her new waitressing job. Apparently it was going as well as could be expected.

I'm hungry on new levels, I replied.

Hilarious.

Payback for all the bee jokes, I said.

What are you doing?

Letting Lottie chauffer me.

Hashtag best big brother, she sent.

I'm gunning hard for the big-family awards show this year.

Good thing you're the one who makes the awards and also the host, she said.

Excellent planning on my part.

Got to get back to work. People aren't going to mess up their orders themselves. Hashtag looking for the big tip.

I would give you all my monies, I told her.

...that might be illegal. But I'd still take it. Have fun with Lottie. XO.

XO, I replied.

"Look at you, all dreamy," Lottie said.

"You're not supposed to be looking at me. You're supposed to be staring at the road in firm concentration," I said.

"Firm concentration. You sound like Mom," Lottie replied. She darted me a look. "Speaking of, what's up with you and Mom?"

"What do you mean?" I hedged.

"You're acting all cagey around her and I see her staring at you with the concerned face she usually reserves for Joel and Jonah," she said.

I sighed. So it wasn't my imagination that things had been weird with Mom, that I'd been on her worried parent radar. "It's nothing."

"I'm supposed to be stepping up here as your closest sibling. Would you tell Haven?"

I sighed again. "She's not happy about me and Bellamy."

"What?" she exclaimed, shocked. "How could anyone not be happy about that? It's like a dream come true."

"I agree," I said.

"It makes no sense," Lottie continued, shaking her head in confusion.

There was no way to tell Lottie Mom's concerns without spilling Bellamy's secret, something I would never do. "Haven thinks it's a mother/son thing."

Lottie grimaced. "That's creepy, but I guess I see it. Jonah and Joel are hopeless."

"We all agree on that."

"So the pressure's on you. Maybe too much pressure. Maybe mom's afraid if you guys break up it will mess things up with all the Browns."

"We won't break up," I said, tone vehement.

"Lots of people break up, nearly everyone. Especially when you start dating in high school. I mean, who marries their high school sweetheart?"

"Uh, Mom and Dad. And look at Haven and Sutton."

"Yeah, look at them. Do you really think they'll stay together?"

"Lottie," I exclaimed.

"I'm serious here, Huntley. They seem mismatched to me."

"They're not mismatched at all. They're perfect," I argued.

"Someone's been drinking the Kool-Aid," she said.

"No, someone's spent a ton of time with them, observing their relationship. I'm telling you, they're solid. Sutton keeps a lid on Haven's crazy ambition. Haven pulls Sutton out of himself, pushes him to connect with other people."

"If you say so," she said, still sounding unconvinced.

"Yeesh, what happened to you? You're pretty cynical for a fifteen-year-old kid."

"I've seen things," she said, sounding otherworldly.

I thought of Bellamy and the things she'd seen, the way she'd been a victim of someone older and in charge. "What kind of things?" I demanded, tone harsh with suspicion. A lot of girls were prey. Bad enough it had happened to my girlfriend. I might actually lose my head if I found out it happened to my sister, too.

Lottie laughed. "Settle, big brother. I was joking. Boys are stupid, present company excluded. I'm just over it. I have my music, and that's enough."

"You sound like me last year."

"Nah, you were naïve. I'm much more cynical," Lottie said.

"What is wrong with my sisters?" I mused. "So skeptical and pragmatic."

"It's the way of the world, Huntley. Most guys aren't nice. Bellamy is lucky to have you, really. I hope she knows."

"I'm lucky to have her, too," I said. I knew that even more after spending the year at public high school. Despite the trauma of her past, Bellamy was well rounded, deep, intelligent, funny, warm, and soft. Not a combination I'd encountered much, and especially not in other girls our age. She cared deeply about other people, about truth, beauty, the future. Truly, she was one in a billion.

"Do you think Parker will come over tonight?"

I shot her a look. "You don't like Parker, do you?"

She darted me a look of disgust. "As if. Parker's younger than I am, on the inside. Any girl who sets her sights on him is in for a world of heartache. He's just funny. We make each other laugh."

I regarded her, eyes narrowed in suspicion, searching for any hidden subtext. "Keep it that way. Parker is nice and, as you said, fun. But that's all. He's not ready for the likes of you."

"I know," Lottie agreed.

We drove in comfortable silence before she spoke again.

"Hot, though."

I didn't have to pretend to gag. The thought of my little sister being into one of my friends was repulsive on a number of levels. "Are you ready for work on Monday?"

She wrinkled her nose at me.

"What? I thought you'd be excited. Haven and I couldn't wait to start." Our dad brought us all into the family car wash business at a certain age. We didn't have to remain in it; there was zero disappointment that Haven and I were choosing our own paths. But while we lived at home, it was our (well paid) responsibility to help out. This year Lottie would take over Haven's job. Together, we would collect the money from the washes and restock supplies. Haven and I had a handy system where I gathered the money as she restocked the soaps and waxes. I assumed it would be the same with Lottie.

"I guess. I don't really want to take time away from my music," Lottie replied. Said by anyone else it would be funny, because how good could a fifteen year old be? In Lottie's case, the answer was *amazing*. None of us had any doubt she would someday go pro, was heading there already. The big question mark in her life was whether she would go straight into music or head to college for more education first.

We rode in silence a few more minutes before she broke it again. "How much does Dad make?"

"He won't say for certain. Based on what I collected from the washes, times the number of washes, I'd say he rakes in about thirty million a year."

Her eyes bugged and the wheel jerked slightly when she twitched.

"That's a raw number, obviously. He has to pay taxes, utilities, employee salaries, insurance. There are a lot of expenditures involved with the washes, more than you probably realize."

"How much do you think he makes after all that stuff?"

I blew out a breath, doing some quick calculations in my head. "Maybe about five million."

"Whoa," Lottie said, breathless and shocked.

Despite growing up with an enormous amount of wealth and privilege, we weren't ignorant of money or what things cost. Our parents gave us an allowance from a young age, helped us save and give, made us do an expenditures report and mock taxes. We knew the value of a dollar, we Mulligans. Money was a big part of our homeschool curriculum. Our parents encouraged each of us to earn our keep, not only with chores, but with anything extra we made from our hobbies. I sold honey from my bees. It wasn't enough to retire, but I'd used the proceeds to buy a few stocks. Haven liked to tease me about being a day trader, but she'd done seamstress jobs for people and invested her own money.

"I'm never going to have that kind of money, as a musician," Lottie said, sounding worried.

"Probably none of us will. Even as a doctor I won't come close to that."

"Well, Joel and Jonah might," Lottie added. Our oldest brothers had decided to go into the family business. Jonah helped run the office with dad while Joel enjoyed the actual construction and physical labor involved in building and setting up the washes. Neither of them had gone to college, nor had any plans to in their future. I couldn't tell if this was a relief or a worry to my parents, neither of whom went to college, both of whom encouraged intellectual pursuits. Though my mom had left my future up to me, I could tell she was not so secretly delighted in my decision to pursue medicine. That was probably another strike against Bellamy, the fear that she might derail me from my goals. Mom should know Bellamy better than that, though. The girl had plans and dreams of her own.

That night as I slid into bed, Bellamy texted. *School starts tomorrow for me.*

Work starts tomorrow for me, I returned. I'd be working more hours this year. I planned to do a lot of reading, but it would be odd not to have classes for the first time since I was five. I didn't actually enjoy the freedom of that. I was a person who thrived on structure.

Preemptively exhausted by life, Bellamy texted.

I bit my lip, staring at the phone. That didn't sound like her. *Everything okay?*

In the long run, yes. Kind of tired. Waitressing life.

I tried to imagine running around a crowded restaurant for six hours, carrying food, taking orders, catering to people's whims while smelling like food. I could see how that would be tiring. *Pretend I'm there hugging you.*

I already was, she replied with a smiley face. *Sometimes I wish we could fast forward through all the hard work preparation for real life, and get to the real life part. Being a kid is...hard.*

It was difficult for me to know how to respond because I'd never minded being a kid. Unlike some others, including Haven, I had never strived for independence. I liked having my life ordered. I had always enjoyed the structure of school during the day, hobbies at night, work in the summer. But I also had my own room in my own gigantic house and my parents would pay for my college. Bellamy was stuck in a kind of in between, still sharing a room with two of her sisters while trying to do the hard work of making money for life and college. No wonder she felt the need to get away somewhere where she was one or the other, either a real kid or a real grownup.

Next year it will be better, I assured her.

Maybe, but I'll have to work next year, too.

I bit my lip. Next year I wouldn't work while attending school. My parents would pay for my college, and I'd rely on my savings for all the extras. Bellamy would be on scholarship with loans. She'd have to supplement that by working as much as possible. *Maybe my parents can adopt you,* I suggested, trying and failing to lighten the mood.

Pretty sure your mom would say no to that.

I sighed at my phone. We were apparently back to that. I wondered if we would ever move beyond it. My phone beeped with another text.

I'm sorry. I'm tired and grumpy and feeling a little overwhelmed by life at the moment. Probably better if I say goodnight and try for a better attitude tomorrow.

Sleep well, I told her. I thought that was the end of it, but my phone beeped a minute later.

What's a bee's favorite novel? She didn't wait for me to reply before finishing the joke. *The Great Gats-bee.*

I love you, terrible jokes and all.

She sent me a smiley face, and I went to bed the same as that face, smiling.

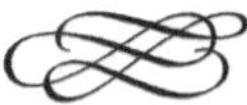

CHAPTER 26

Bellamy was busy. In preparation for next year, she planned her hardest curriculum yet, lots of high level history, literature, and of course Latin. She worked whenever she wasn't studying, meaning she hadn't been exaggerating about the difficulty of her life at the moment. I felt bad for her but, aside from offering tutoring she didn't actually need, I had no idea how to help.

And it made me feel worse that, in comparison, my life was so easy. It was that guilt, combined with a desire to get a jump on my career, that led me to a second job at the hospital. I would be heading up a team of other kids like me, medicine minded kids who wanted a taste of real life experience before college or careers. Some of them were also doing community service, a sort of penance for crimes they'd committed. It was a strange combo of kids who actually wanted to be there, who were enthusiastic about spending time in a hospital running errands, and kids who hated every minute, who tried to sneak away and slack off.

I had never managed anyone before. It was a new and disconcerting experience to be in charge of other people, especially when I still saw everyone as being in charge of me. Before this year, Haven had managed pretty much everything in our lives. She was that type of person—

driven, competitive, and focused. I was a floater, happy to tag along wherever she led. Except now I was apparently an authority figure. The diversion from my regular life was enough to give me whiplash.

I have so much to learn, I thought, as I stared at my new team.

I know nothing, Bellamy texted me at almost the same moment. She was taking a college class, her first, and it was her first day.

Same. Hashtag real life together, one day at a time.

That's a terrible hashtag, but I'll take it, she replied.

Bee happy, I told her.

I'm trying, she returned. I frowned at the phone, sensing she wasn't as okay as she pretended to be. One of these days I'd have to see her in person, to assure myself she was okay. But so far the past week our free time hadn't lined up. When I was free, she was working. When she was free, I was working.

"So, like, we're supposed to find something to do, right?" A girl named Michelle stared at me in disdain as I snapped to attention and shoved my phone back in my pocket.

"No, we wait here until they call us to run things around the hospital. We'll be delivering charts or people or supplies," I told her.

"Great, downtime with my thoughts," she said, rolling her eyes. She rested her head on her doubled fists and stared blankly at the desk.

I wasn't privy to which of my team was there voluntarily and which was there under court order. If I had to guess about Michelle, I'd say it was the latter. Then again, maybe she was merely impatient.

"Was that your girlfriend on the phone? You had a doofy smile on your face."

"Yes, that was my girlfriend," I said.

"How long have you been together?" she asked.

"Two months."

"Won't last," Michelle said, now swiveling to stare at the desk again.

"Of course it will," I returned.

She laughed. "What are you, like the last romantic on earth? Of course it won't. No one does at this stage. One of you will mess it up, big time."

"No, I've known her forever."

"That will make the screw up worse," Michelle said.

I frowned, not liking that thought at all. "It's not like that. Bellamy and I are solid, we're above all the high school drama."

"That's what everyone says, and then they break up," she said, rolling her eyes.

"What is it with girls these days?" I groused. "So cynical. Where have all the princesses gone?"

"We got tired of waiting for our princes to rescue us and gave up, realizing we're going to have to rescue ourselves," Michelle said.

She tried to say it offhandedly, but it fell flat, betraying some private hurt or disappointment. I stared at her, thinking it was probably true, and how sad was that? "I'm not like that," I said.

Michelle turned to regard me. "You're probably not. Probably why you're already taken."

"You have to have faith that things will work out for you, too," I encouraged.

She shot me an eyebrow upraised in irritation. "Really? My own dad doesn't want anything to do with me. Why would some random guy?"

"I…" I had no answer, and I sort of hated it. My world thus far had been completely sheltered. I had basked in the love and care and comfort of my wealthy, adoring family. How was I to answer people like Michelle?

"Mm-hmm," she said, facing forward again to stare at the desk.

Thankfully a call came and she ran a file to the fifth floor, giving me a reprieve from my deep and disturbing thoughts. Why couldn't anything be easy? I thought of my mom, leaning on my dad outside Sutton's dorm room. *Why is everything so hard all the time?*

Suddenly I wanted to go back to being a kid again, where everything was safe and easy. Was I actually prepared for real life where everything was apparently bleak and terrifying? What if all the love I'd taken for granted had done nothing but make me too soft to survive outside it?

I pulled out my phone and stared at a list of inspiring quotes I'd been compiling from people I admired. One from Winston Churchill popped out at me. "When you're going through hell, keep going."

I put my phone back in my pocket and stared at the desk. Maybe the key to life wasn't how easy or hard you had it, but how many times you kept going despite all that. The thought gave me some comfort because it meant I wasn't a hopeless victim of circumstance. Neither was Michelle. Neither was Bellamy. We were all on a journey, and we all had to keep moving forward. And if I could make some-one's journey a little better, I would.

That was probably why I was smiling when Michelle returned, to inject a little kindness into her world. She, however, took one look at my face and rolled her eyes, groaning.

"You're, like, an optimist or something, aren't you?"

"I guess so," I replied.

"Figures." She slouched into the chair beside me, rested her chin on her fists, and resumed staring at the desk.

T wo days later, Bellamy and I finally saw each other in person. We went out for supper and then, unable to think of anything else to do, sat in my basement and tried to talk while an endless stream of my siblings trailed in and out.

"I have to work the next four days in a row and I have three papers due for my two college classes, not to mention the other stuff I'm taking," Bellamy said. She rested her head on the back of the couch and closed her eyes.

"I wish I could help you somehow," I said, feeling vaguely guilty over my lack of life stress. I had no classes to take, and even my two jobs seemed to pale in comparison. So far my partnership with Lottie was working as well as the one with Haven. The only difference was that she asked me what to do instead of telling. It was a switch to lead instead of follow, but I was becoming more comfortable with the role.

"You are. I just feel bad for being such a complainer," she said, sighing in delight when I picked up her hand and began to massage it.

"Stating fact is not complaining. You have a lot going on right now."

"My friend, Jenna, has been giving me a hard time for ditching her, and so has Dylan. It's hard to find time for everything and everyone. Especially when I mostly just want to be with you. But then I have this warning voice telling me I shouldn't be that girl who spends all my free time with my boyfriend, to the exclusion of everything else."

"How can we mute that voice?" I asked, and she giggled.

"It's true, though. Everything is so easy with you, so fun. Makes me feel like we're doing something wrong for the lack of drama."

"I'm not so much with the drama," I reminded her.

"One of my very favorite things about you," she said, reaching out blindly, eyes still closed. She attempted to pat my stomach, missed, and patted the edge of my elbow instead.

"Come on, you're low drama, too."

"I try to be, but, being female, it's hard not to get sucked in. Things with other girls are wacky. Be glad you're male."

"I am," I said, nodding. Girls seemed to have it much harder, in all the ways.

"Me, too, come to think of it," she said. She opened her eyes and circled my neck, smiling up at me. "Let's do something fun my next day off."

"Like what?"

"Surprise me," she said.

"I've been thinking of starting a new hive. I guess you could help me with that," I suggested.

She poked me. "Maybe I'd better plan it. We could go hiking some-where. It would be like a throwback to weather camp."

"So would copious amounts of time spent making out," I said.

"I'm game for that, too," she said, eyes dropping to my lips.

"Oh, Bellamy. Hi, I didn't know you were here."

I didn't think my mom was lying, but she almost never came to the basement. I looked around and realized it was void of anyone besides Bellamy and me. And now my mom. Alone time at our house was so rare it was hard not to be suspicious over the interruption.

"Hi," Bellamy said, withdrawing awkwardly from my embrace. We hadn't done anything more than hug, but I knew she still felt bad about it, as if we'd been caught. I knew because I felt the same, and I didn't like it. I was eighteen and a high school graduate. Why was my mom hovering?

"I was looking for Margaret. She wanted me to braid her hair before 4H."

"Haven't seen her," I said. Not to say she hadn't been in the basement, just that I was used to ignoring my siblings.

"Okay, if you see her, tell her I'm in the kitchen," Mom said. Since the kitchen was pretty much her lair, it was a safe bet Margaret would find her as soon as she looked for her.

"Okay," I replied. I stared at her while she stared at us. Bellamy shrunk into herself while I felt like I expanded, blocking her from my *mother*, of all people.

"So," Mom drawled, glancing at the stairs. "Well, I guess I'll go." Finally, she turned and went back upstairs, ending our misery.

"That was fun," I said, staring after my mom in perplexed silence.

"Did she do that kind of stuff with Haven and Sutton?"

"I don't know. I was usually with them, so I don't know that she felt the need. I guess we'd better expect one of my buffer siblings at any moment."

"Then we'd better make the most of this opportunity," Bellamy said. She grabbed me and kissed me with something that felt a whole lot like anger. And while I realized the anger was directed at my mother, I didn't mind, not even a little.

"She should check up on us more often," I said between kisses, my lips moving against hers.

"Less talking, more frantic panic kissing," Bellamy instructed, yanking me closer.

"Oh, so this is why Mom called me from my room and sent me

downstairs," Lottie said, poking her head around the corner. "No, please, carry on as if I'm not here." She came the rest of the way down the stairs and curled up in a chair with her guitar. "Mood music."

Bellamy laughed and snuggled in beside me as we tuned in to listen to Lottie play and sing. Or at least I tuned in. When I glanced down a minute later at Bellamy, she was asleep.

CHAPTER 27

A week later, my mom woke me from a dead sleep.

"Huntley."

I sat up, confused and befuddled, as I always was in the middle of the night. Some people struggled with insomnia; I was not one of them. "Wha...?" What time was it? What day was it? What *year* was it?

"Brooke called. It's Bellamy. She's in the hospital. Get dressed."

There was something especially ominous in my mom's tone, I would realize later. I threw on clothes, I had no idea what, but later it turned out to be jeans and a hoodie I thought Haven stole and took to college with her. She must have tucked it into my drawer before she left. In any case, I was dressed far sloppier than usual, but I didn't care.

"What happened?" I asked my mom as soon as we piled in the car. She drove, another anomaly. Since I turned sixteen, I had taken over all driving when the two of us were together without my dad or older brothers.

Mom shook her head.

"Car accident?" I tried again, my glance falling to the clock. She should have gotten home from work hours ago. Did something happen?

My mom shook her head again.

"Mom, please, give me something." The panic in my tone finally snapped her to reality.

"She's on a psych hold," Mom said without looking at me. We were on a deserted stretch of roadway, so I knew it wasn't for driving purposes that she didn't tear her eyes away from the street. There was a fair amount of I-told-you-so in her tone. If she spoke it out loud, I wasn't certain I'd be able to forgive her. Thankfully she pressed her lips together and kept driving.

We made the remainder of the trip in tense silence. A psych hold. What did that mean? "Will I be allowed to see her?"

"Brooke asked me to bring you. I'm doing this for *her*."

I stuffed my reply deep inside. She should be doing it for Bellamy, not her mother's long friendship. Because Bellamy was my girlfriend and I cared about her. Because it was the right thing to do in the situation.

"Huntley," she began again, tone heavy, but I didn't want to hear it.

"Not now," I snapped, then added, "please," as I remembered what my dad would make of the conversation. The number one thing he wouldn't tolerate in our house was rudeness or disrespect to our mother.

Mom nodded once and gripped the wheel tighter. We finished the trip in quiet, but not the comforting kind. My stomach churned, my palms sweated. Had Bellamy tried to hurt herself in some way? I just talked to her a few hours ago. She was having a stressful night at work, but they'd all been stressful lately. Her boss was nitpicky and unlikeable, and she wasn't the only one who'd felt that way. One of the other waitresses walked out just tonight, leaving them short handed, doubling her workload. Would that be reason to do whatever she'd done? Or, worse, was it me? Had I inadvertently done something? Not paid enough attention?

"We're here," Mom said, making me realize we'd been sitting in the parking lot a couple of minutes while I stared blankly through the front windshield. "You don't have to go in, if you don't want to. I didn't even ask." She bit her lip, looking uncertain.

"Of course I want to," I said, but gently. Brooke would need Mom's support; she shouldn't have to worry about me, too.

Mom gave a nod and we left the car. I towered over her now, which was still new enough to be odd. She was my *mom*. Wasn't she supposed to be the big one? But I'd passed her up by my fifteenth birthday, now by a wide margin. Someday we'd probably be like that book, *I'll Love You Forever*, with me in the role of her caregiver. I began to see why that dumb book always made her cry.

We stepped onto the elevator and I attempted to draw a deep breath but the air was still and dry. Or maybe it was my lungs. Maybe they didn't work when I was this nervous and tense. Mom gave my bicep a reassuring squeeze, and it was nice, that little moment of, *I'm still your mom, and everything is going to be okay.* Those moments and reassurances came less and less these days.

As soon as we located the correct hallway, Brooke launched herself at Mom, crying hard. I stood helplessly by, shifting from foot to foot, uncertain what to do. Finally Mom nudged me with her head in the direction of the room Brooke had left. I faced it, feeling a little lost and a lot alone. What would I find on the other side. *Bellamy.* No matter what state she was in, I had to see her.

That realization propelled me forward, in a hurry now. I pushed through the door and saw her lying in a bed that looked way too big, her gaze toward the window. She looked pale and wan and—worse— lacking her usual sparkle. She turned at the sound of me, flinched, and then put her hands over her face and started to cry.

"I'm so sorry," she said between heaving sobs. I went forward, eased onto the bed, and drew her close against my chest. She let go of her face and clutched me instead, wadding my shirt in her hands as she wet it with a gallon of tears. "I'm sorry, I'm so, so sorry." It seemed to be all she could say.

I held her and rubbed her back, letting her tears play themselves out. Having sisters was definitely good for a lot. It had taught me how to comfortably deal with crying females. That information alone was priceless. I didn't speak, didn't ask questions, didn't try to stop the endless torrent. I simply held on and let it happen.

After a while the tears came to an end. She sagged against me, exhausted. "What happened?" I finally asked.

She took a shaky breath and let it out slowly. "Nothing."

The absurdity of the situation hit us and we both laughed. She eased back, using her sleeve to dab at her eyes. "It all got blown out of proportion. I...I've been stressed, you know that. Lots going on."

I nodded encouragingly. She reached across me for a tissue, dabbed some more, and continued. "After the...after camp that year, when everything came out, I started seeing a therapist. It seemed to help, so much that last year I stopped seeing her. Yay, I'm cured." She dabbed dramatically at her tears, motioning around the hospital, and we laughed again.

"Later I'm going to feel bad for finding this funny," I told her.

She shook her head. "Don't, because it is, and I need to laugh at it. Anyway, I stopped therapy and soon after that we started dating."

I tensed. "Is this my fault? This, er, reversal."

"Reversal," she said, snorting. "I don't think you reverse to being crazy. And, no, it is absolutely not your fault. I love being with you, you know that. It's been a lot of pressure from a lot of different sources and some memories have been coming back, memories of things I thought I'd already worked through. Tonight I got home from my long, miserable night of work, smelling like fried food, as usual. So I got into the shower and...this memory." She pressed her lips together and gave me a look filled with so much raw pain. I was torn between sadness on her behalf and anger on my own. I wanted to hunt down her abuser and make him pay for all the ways he'd hurt her. Instead I reached out and rubbed her back again.

She took another shaky breath. "It was a memory from that camp, one I'd pushed so far down I had completely forgotten. The...guy, he had a private cabin with a private bath. The shower...I'd forgotten." She shook her head and shuddered hard. "Anyway, I sort of...went away while I was showering tonight. My mom found me sobbing, lying on the floor, cold water making me shiver. When she asked me what was wrong, I said..." she sucked another breath, this one the shakiest of all. "I said I wanted to die, that I was so tired of dealing with everything. The second part is true, I'm so tired of dealing with everything. But I don't actually want to die. I said it in the moment, blowing off stress and steam. But with my history, with everything, Mom totally freaked out and called my old therapist. They both agreed I should come here to be assessed." She put her hand over her eyes. "I'm so humiliated."

I remained quiet, searching for the right way to answer, for the perfect thing to say that wouldn't mess things up more. In the end I went with, "I'm sorry. I'm so sorry you're going through this. I wish I could help."

"You can't, though. What we had was so great. If it couldn't help, nothing can."

It took me a few beats to catch the past tense. "What are you saying?"

"I'm saying obviously we can't be together anymore. Your mom is right, Huntley. I'm a total train wreck. If this keeps going, it's only going to hurt you more." She was crying again, silently and gently this time. I was on the verge of it myself.

"No," I said dismissively, trying to brush aside her words. "We are not breaking up over this; we are not breaking up over anything."

"Look, I know how you are."

"How am I?" I asked, feeling my first prickle of irritation.

"Loyal. Steady. Once your mind is made up, you stick with it, especially when it's a person. You've decided on me, but you can't. You have to undo it. You have to un-decide. I'm not...I'm not healthy, and I'm certainly not stable. I'm a walking catastrophe."

"Stop saying that," I said, letting go of her to cover my ears.

She sighed and rested her head on my shoulder, sagging against me. I took that as a good sign that maybe she'd relented and dropped my hands, putting one arm around her and cinching her closer.

"I'm going to miss you," she said softly.

I rolled my eyes and gave her a squeeze. "No, you're not. Know why? Because I'm not going anywhere. This is a bad night, a bad moment, but that's all it is. A blip."

"I hardly think my mental health is a blip," she said.

"You know what I mean. Do not let one moment of our lives define us or our relationship. We all go through things."

"Really? When is the last time you were in the psych ward?" she asked. She was annoyed, but I was encouraged. Spitfire Bellamy was much more like the original than the sad, hopeless creature she'd been on my arrival.

"Give it time, I'm only eighteen," I said which, as I intended, made her sputter a laugh and shove my shoulder. I pulled her legs into my lap and leaned back against the bed. She copied my pose, staring into my face.

"I love you."

"I love you, too," I said, ignoring the way her statement sounded like a benediction.

"Which is why we're breaking up," she continued undaunted.

"We're not breaking up. It takes two people to break up and I don't agree, therefore, we're not breaking up," I said.

She rolled her eyes. "We're not married."

"Yet."

"We don't both have to agree to break up. I can do it on my own, and I am."

I shook my head.

"Huntley," she said, annoyed. She tried to withdraw her legs, but I held on to them.

"Leave them, I'm cold. You're a human blanket."

"Stop being charming when I'm trying to dump you," she said.

"Stop trying to dump me because you're embarrassed about being in the loony bin," I said, smiling when she giggled and pressed her hand over her mouth.

"Please, you have to let me do this," she said, becoming serious once more.

"Nope," I said, shaking my head.

She was getting huffy again. She frowned at me. "I need to focus on my mental health."

"Great, I'll drive you to therapy," I said.

"It doesn't work like that. It takes a lot of energy and focus to try and fix stuff. You, while adorable and pleasant, take a lot of mental and emotional energy I need in order to do the hard work I need to do."

I put up my hand and mimed a puppet speaking. "Blah, blah, blah, trying to use guilt to break up with you, blah, blah."

She frowned harder. I knew better than to laugh, but I was tempted.

"What else do you have, counselor?" I asked her.

She faced forward, arms crossed and thinking. When she faced me again, she was calm. "You don't believe in soul mates."

"No, but you knew that when we got together. You can't make it a deal breaker now," I said.

"I'm not. You are."

"What?"

"If you don't believe we're meant to be together, if you believe you can be with anyone who shares proximity, then you have to let me go. You will find someone else with the appropriate proximity."

"And what will you do?" I countered, getting annoyed again. "Find another soul mate?"

She shook her head. "If I can't be with you, I can't be with anyone. So I won't. I'll get on with my career, focus on friendships and travel. It was what I intended to do before you came along anyway."

"Your grand plan is to become a cat lady?" I asked.

"I'm a dog person, but yes. I can't do this, can't meld my life with someone else's. I tried, and I can't."

"This giving up? That's not trying. That's quitting."

"No, it's throwing in the towel before things get worse. What happens a decade from now? Are you going to drag our kids along to the psych ward?"

"You have no idea what will happen ten years from now, if this will still even be an issue. Maybe you'll work through everything. But if not, I don't care. And, yes, I will bring our kids along, if that's what it takes to support you when you're dealing with something difficult."

"Huntley." She pressed her fingers to her temple. "You cannot be okay with this."

"I'm not. I hate seeing you hurting, hate that you're trying to push me away. But I also know why you're doing it, and it's not going to work. You're scared, I get that. But fear isn't a reason to run away and hide."

"Easy for you to say when you're not the one falling apart," she said and started to cry again. "Look at me. I can't even stop leaking for five minutes to have a rational conversation. This is not right, and it's not normal. You don't want any part of this."

"Why don't you let me decide what I do and do not want?" I said.

"*I* don't want you to have any part of this. This is embarrassing. No, it's mortifying. You are so healthy and solid and amazing. It's shameful and humiliating for me that you have to see me like this, that you have to show up in the middle of the night at the hospital and give me a pep talk and loving reassurances. I shouldn't need that. I don't like it, and I don't want it."

"Well, that's dumb," I said, now crossing my arms over my chest.

"Yes, it is. It's everything bad in the universe, but there it is," she agreed.

"If you were diabetic or had cancer, would you be ashamed of needing insulin or chemo?"

She shook her head.

"So how is this different? It's mental health, and it's part of you."

"Maybe in a perfect world it wouldn't be different, but we don't live in a perfect world. We live in a world where having mental health issues is stigmatizing. If you don't believe me, ask your mother how she felt about bringing you here, how she feels about the continuation of our relationship."

"Leave my mom out of this. She has nothing to do with this," I said.

"She has everything to do with it because she's right. Don't you get that? She sees me, the real me as I am inside, and she's trying to protect you. You shouldn't be mad at her, you should listen to her and run away. Far and fast and with my blessing." She uncrossed her arms and flung them wide for emphasis.

Even pale and wan and embarrassed and broken, she was so beautiful. "How bad would it be if we're making out when our moms enter the room?"

She froze and then burst into my favorite giggle and covered her mouth. "Huntley." Her tone was longsuffering. She rested her head on the bed again and regarded me with a serious expression. I mimicked her, except I was smiling instead.

"I can't help it. I love you, and you're pretty."

"I'm not. I finished the world's worst shower and didn't even comb my hair." She held up a clump of her hair, which I now realized was tangled and limp.

"At least you're clean," I said.

She chuckled again before pushing it away. "Stop trying to bright side my breakdown."

"What's black and yellow and flies at three thousand feet?" I said.

She shook her head, refusing to answer.

"A bee in an airplane."

She let loose a little laugh and pushed it back down again. "I love you, but you have to go away."

I shook my head.

"You can't ignore things and pretend they're going to go away. This isn't going to stop. I'm not suddenly going to be well and healed from my past abuse. This is something that's going to be with me, maybe for the rest of my life."

"Okay," I said.

"You can't be okay with this," she yelled.

"I can, and I am," I declared.

"You're living in la-la land," she said, poking my chest.

"Uh, I'm not the one in the mental unit," I said, grinning when she huffed.

"You should be."

"Probably."

She rested her head on my shoulder again. "Seriously, no one is as mentally fit as you seem. It's disconcerting."

"I know, baby." I kissed the top of her head.

She snuggled closer. "I'm so tired."

"Go to sleep. I'm here."

"Will you...will you hold me?" she asked, tone so tentative and uncertain my heart broke all over again.

"Forever and ever," I said, easing my arms around her and pulling her close. She nestled again and, a few minutes later, she was asleep.

CHAPTER 28

When my mom and Brooke poked their heads into the room a while later, Bellamy was still asleep, cradled in my embrace. My mom pressed her lips together. If she kept doing that the blood was going to leave them forever. In contrast, Brooke melted at the sight of us, going a little weepy and gooey.

"I'm so glad she has you," she whispered, using her sleeve to dab her eyes.

I glanced down at Bellamy, not only to break the awkwardness, but because I didn't want Bellamy to wake up.

"Once she's out, she's out," Brooke added.

"We should probably go. I need to get breakfast for the others," my mom said.

Brooke jumped to attention and hugged her. "Of course. Thanks for coming. Love you."

"Love you, too," Mom said sincerely while I extricated myself from Bellamy. Free of my clasp, she curled into a little ball. I covered her with the blanket and touched my hand to her head. Leaving was hard. When she woke, she would rehash everything. What would happen without me there to reassure her?

"I'm staying," Brooke said, making me wonder if she could read my mind somehow. Probably the same way my own mom could do it. She folded into the recliner beside the bed, staring at Bellamy as I turned and faced my mom.

We walked in silence to the car. Maybe I could read my mom's mind, too, because I was pretty certain I knew what she was thinking. *This is why I didn't want you to date her. This is exactly what I was afraid of. It's too much, too soon. Danger. Break up, move on.*

Thankfully she didn't say any of it. But her expression was pinched, her posture tight. And she drove, something else that told me she was upset.

I rode in the passenger seat feeling small and helpless and frustrated. Why couldn't my mom see how amazing Bellamy was, how hard she was trying? Why didn't she see how good we were together, how right for each other?

We pulled into the garage and she shut off the car.

"Mom."

She tensed as if I'd yelled it, even though I purposely kept my tone soft and gentle.

"Yes." Her hands gripped the steering wheel as if gearing up for a fight. I vowed not to give her one, ever cognizant of my dad and his opinion on the matter.

"Do you feel like Dad rescued you?"

She blinked through the front windshield, taken aback. That was clearly not the question she'd been expecting. "Yes, completely. When your dad and I started dating, I was kind of a mess. I mean, you've met your grandparents and aunts and uncles." She tossed me a wry smile. We didn't see her family often for that reason; they were kind of a wreck. "Your dad was so solid and steady, such a rock in my life. It allowed me to grow up, to heal."

"Why won't you let me do that for Bellamy?"

She blinked at me, gripping the wheel tighter. "It's not the same," she croaked.

"Why not?" I asked.

"Because you're a kid," she said.

"I'm older than Dad was, when you two got together," I reminded her.

She frowned and her lower lip quivered. "We're done talking about this," she said. I watched in exhausted dismay as she slipped out of the car and slammed the door. A few beats later, Lottie took her place.

"What'd you do to Mom?" she asked.

"Nothing. Why?"

"She was crying. She and dad closed themselves in his office," she said.

"I didn't do anything, I swear. She's being so unreasonable," I said.

Lottie started the car and I pressed my hand over my eyes. "Lottie, please. I'm so tired. I don't feel like driving right now."

"I know, that's why I'm taking you for pancakes," she said.

I dropped my hands. Pancakes sounded amazing, and it would get me out of the house and away from my parents, two people I had never wanted to get away from before. "Okay."

She tossed me a grin. "Do I know the way to a man's heart or what?"

"Hopefully only your brother's," I scolded.

"So weird and creepy, Huntley," she returned.

"It came out wrong, but you know what I mean," I said.

"You're actually slurring."

"I'm so tired," I said.

"I once heard that how people behave when they're sleep deprived is how they would behave drunk. Looks like you'd be a little slap happy and confused."

"We'll never know," I said. After seeing some of my friends drunk last year, including Sutton, I had zero desire to ever join their ranks.

"You're so good," Lottie said, shaking her head.

"So are you, I hope," I returned.

She shrugged, which was disconcerting, but I was too tired to delve into it.

"Psst, Huntley," Lottie whispered, making me realize I'd fallen asleep. "We're here."

I sat up and wiped the sleep from my face. So much for being a responsible driving instructor. "Okay." I stumbled from the car and toward the restaurant. Parker was already waiting at a table. He waved us over.

"How did you get Parker to wake up this early?" I asked. He was a notorious late sleeper.

"The prospect of pancakes is powerful incentive, my friend."

"True that," I agreed, giving her shoulders a squeeze.

"Mulligans," Parker greeted us with a serious nod that looked all wrong on his never-serious face. "To what do I owe the pleasure of this impromptu pancake parade?"

"Huntley needs cheering," Lottie said. "He's Havenless."

"As are we all," Parker said, tone solemn, head bowed. He pressed his hand over his heart, observing a moment of silence. "Has anyone heard from the lovebirds?" They both looked at me.

"We text every day," I said.

"She doesn't text *me*," Parker said resentfully.

"Me neither," Lottie said, but her tone sounded a little sad, a little wistful. I was beginning to realize how much of our lives Lottie had spent feeling like an outsider. Haven and I had always had each other and we felt entitled to our separateness because we were twins. But there was Lottie, only two years behind us and completely on her own. Who was her other half? Her matching Mulligan? No one, as far as I could tell.

"She's doing predictably well," I said, glossing over the raw emotion from both of them. "She loves her classes, loves being busy, is making new friends."

"And Sutton?" Lottie pressed.

"Is predictably cynical. His classes are filled with, in his words, 'anti-social reprobates.' So far nothing has provided him with any career direction, and he pretty much hates most people in his dorm. He's spent all of his weekends with Haven and seems to like her friends, which is good. I think we're going to see a far more reclusive and subdued Sutton than we knew in high school."

"That seems more like him," Parker said. "The party guy persona always felt a bit contrived and forced, if I'm being honest."

"Why are you being honest and sensible? You need coffee," Lottie said, pushing the carafe toward him. He took it with a smile, tossing her a wink as he poured.

"And what about you, Huntley? How's your world?" Parker asked. I agreed with Lottie, it was disconcerting when he turned all serious and earnest, like a psychiatrist or something. I was too used to the Puckish Parker to accept anything different.

"It's...okay. My mom's not happy about the Bellamy situation. Kind of hard."

"You Mulligans are parent pleasers. I keep telling you that you need to get over that. Once you throw off the fetters of parental involvement, all your problems will be solved," he said.

"Really?" Lottie asked.

"No," he said, dropping the happy-go-lucky façade once more. "But you find ways to stop caring so much and numb the pain." He tipped his coffee to her and took another sip.

"That's the thing, I do care what Mom thinks. But I also think she's wrong. How is it possible to feel both things? To love and respect her and also believe she doesn't understand?" I asked.

"Because, spoiler alert, Mom is human, too. Sometimes she *is* wrong. I guess the trick is to really try and figure out if this is one of those times. Is she?" Lottie asked, tipping her head to probe my eyes when I tried to avoid contact. I squirmed a little under her gaze.

"It feels weird and wrong to go against Mom and Dad. But I love Bellamy. I honestly believe we're good together."

"Maybe you should take a little time apart," Lottie suggested.

I shot her a wounded look of utter betrayal.

She put up her hands in surrender. "For your sake, as much as hers. If you guys are really meant to be, you'll come back together, don't you think?"

"I thought you didn't believe in destiny," I reminded her.

"Neither do you," she returned. "But you believe in persistence, loyalty, and commitment. All of those things would be needed to stay together during a separation."

"Separation seems stupid," I said, feeling panicky over the thought.

How could we possibly sustain a relationship if we were apart? Especially with so many factors working to pull us away? My mom, Bellamy's mental script, our busyness. To me it seemed like a recipe for disaster. But if we took some time to think about things, it would prove to my mom we were more serious than two dumb teenagers. And it would give Bellamy the time she needed to work on her health.

"Maybe it is. I don't have any answers. I'm trying to be a supportive sounding board," Lottie said.

"You Mulligans are so darn adorable and saintly," Parker said, regarding us with a smile.

"No, we're not," Lottie and I said together.

"And here comes the irresistible Mulligan humility. It's too much," Parker said, holding up his hands as if to ward us away.

"Shut it," Lottie said, tossing a wadded napkin at him. He caught it and tossed it back to her. Beside us, an old woman gave us the stink eye for being disruptive.

"Children," I said mildly.

"Uh-oh, Dad's getting mad," Parker whispered, and Lottie snorted. "You know what you need? A night out with Parker. Let's go out tonight. We'll do something fun."

"Something Parker fun or something Huntley fun?" I clarified.

He grimaced. "I am not feeding your bees or checking your windsock."

Lottie snorted a laugh, covering her mouth with her hand.

"And I am not getting drunk or ending the night at the house of some random guy named Chuck because his parents are out of town," I returned.

Parker picked up his phone and pretended to text. "Can't make it tonight, Chuck. Going out with scared old man."

"There has to be a compromise between my old mannishness and your frat boyishness," I said. We'd never been able to find it, but I assumed it existed.

Lottie raised her hand. "There is, and here I am. You're both invited to my gig tonight. There will be music and food and other people under the age of twenty five in attendance."

"You had me at food," Parker said.

"Sounds good," I replied, feeling vaguely guilty again. A good brother would automatically go to all his sister's performances. But Lottie had so many, multiple nights a week and on most weekends. It was a little hard to keep track. Honestly, I wondered if anyone in the family went. How had Lottie gotten so swept under the rug in our big family?

"Will you set me up with one of your friends?" Parker asked.

"Sure. Fair warning, all of them are guys," she said.

"Yes, but are they hot?" Parker returned and she threw another napkin at him.

CHAPTER 29

How are you?

I waited to text Bellamy until my mom told me she was home from the hospital. I wasn't certain if she was allowed to have her phone before then.

Good. Tired. Embarrassed. Overwhelmed.

All but the embarrassed part can stay. There is nothing to be embarrassed over, I assured her.

There's a lot, actually. I don't know anyone else who has ever been on a psych hold. Do you?

I know a lot of people who should have been, I answered sincerely. *A lot of people who would probably be healthier if they'd reached out and gotten the help they needed.*

You're nice.

So are you.

Want to come over? she offered.

Yes, but Parker and I are going to Lottie's gig. Want to come? She's assured us there will be food.

I'd love to, but my mom has me under freak-out-lock-and-key for a while.

Ah, sorry about that. I'll see you tomorrow?

Sure, she agreed and even with several miles between us I could feel her despair and uncertainty.

I love you, I reminded her.

She didn't reply. I tried to remind myself I was supposed to be giving her space, at her behest, but it was hard when all I wanted to do was swoop in, pick her up, and hold her close. I couldn't fight this battle for her, though. All I could do was come along beside her and offer support. But what was the best way to do that? That was the biggest question in my mind. By giving her space like she said? Or by erasing the space between us and showing up regardless of her words?

Lottie graciously allowed me to drive to her event, mostly because she had her pre-performance buzz going and couldn't stop tapping her fingers on her violin case and rocking back and forth in her seat.

"You look like one of those people who is on something," I said.

"How would you know?" she asked.

"I know things," I said, tone stuffed with big-brother cynicism.

Lottie snorted. "You know nothing. You're as sheltered as I am."

"Hey, I spent an entire year in public school," I defended.

"So? I play shows with those same people every weekend. Believe me, I know more than you do about the real world."

That might be true, and I kind of hated it, so I kept my mouth shut. Note to self: keep a better eye on little sister. "Do you like any of these guys you play with?"

She made a gagging sound. "No, absolutely no. Musicians, man." She shook her head.

"You're a musician," I reminded her.

"I know," she agreed, winding her finger around her ear. "Boy musicians are the worst, so damaged and artistic and misunderstood, but at the same time cocky and remote. It's a potent combination for some girls. You'll see what I'm talking about when you meet the groupies."

"There are groupies?" I asked.

"Hordes of them."

"Do you have groupies?"

"Nah, it doesn't work in reverse. Girl musicians don't have that sort of clout. I'm invisible."

"Thank heavens for small favors," I muttered. Lottie laughed. "Seriously, you shouldn't be dating yet."

"Spoken like a true big brother," she said. "No worries, though. Guys don't see me like that. I'm always the pal, the one who sets them up with other girls."

I didn't have to be a genius to hear the despair in her tone. And while I might secretly rejoice that boys hadn't yet discovered her, I didn't like the amount of dejection I heard. "Lottie, seriously, if a guy doesn't see how amazing you are, it's his loss."

"Spoken like a true big brother," she repeated, this time with an affectionate smile and hair tousle. I shoved her arm away and smoothed my hair. Not that it made much difference. My hair was short and stubbornly well behaved. Wind didn't affect it, and neither did my siblings' teasing.

"Haven wants me to record some of the show so they can see."

"Why? She's seen me play a million times," Lottie said.

"It's good to keep up."

"Park here. You're lucky we're early enough to get a spot. It gets crowded later on."

"That's probably when Parker will show up," I said, but I was wrong. Parker was already inside, chatting up a group of girls who didn't seem interested.

"There's something wrong with them," he said in a whispered aside. "Nothing is working on them."

"I would say it's because they have good taste, but that's not it. They're groupies, here for the musicians," Lottie said, rolling her eyes in disgust at the group of fawning females. They eyed me, probably trying to tell if I was part of the band, and I resisted the urge to back away from their predatory ogling. *Tone deaf,* I wanted to tell them, which wasn't exactly true but close enough. I could carry a tune in the most basic manner but certainly lacked the talent of my sister. As well as the desire to be on stage and perform.

"Man, why didn't I stick with those guitar lessons?" Parker lamented.

"Because you never stick with anything?" Lottie guessed.

"I'm stuck with you," he said. He reached to rifle her hair, but she batted his arm away and punched him in the gut. Having a lot of brothers meant my sisters were pretty good at handling themselves around guys.

"Geez," Parker muttered, pressing both palms to his gut. "Internal bleeding much, Lottie?"

Her response was to giggle maniacally, which made me and Parker smile. "I'd say break a leg, but I'm afraid you'd break mine," he muttered when her set was about to begin. We ambled to a table and sat down. The groupie girls positioned themselves directly in front of the stage as the rest of Lottie's band finished their setting up sound check.

"I've never actually heard her play before," Parker confessed, "except tinkering around the house."

"She's good," I tried to say, but the band started and the words were drowned out. The thing I'd forgotten, the thing I soon remembered, was that Lottie was better than good; Lottie was amazing. She alternated between the guitar, the fiddle, and the mandolin with the ease of someone three times her age who'd been playing forever. There was a guy on lead guitar, who also sang, and a guy on backup guitar, but it was Lottie who stole the show, in my totally non-biased opinion. They were what you'd expect a high school band to sound like. Lottie blew them away. She sounded grownup and professional, and when she sang along on backup, it was hard not to wish she was singing lead instead of the mullet headed guitar guy.

Most reasonable people in the room seemed to agree. Their eyes were on Lottie. Not the groupies, however. They howled for the two guitarists, obscuring the cheers of the crowd as they tried to outdo each other in their attempts to be noticed. Lottie gave me a look like, *You see what I'm dealing with here.*

Wow, I mouthed, allowing my grimace to match my distaste. She laughed and continued her set. I sent Bellamy a text.

Group of insane girls here making me even happier you're mine.

Define insane, she returned.

I sent her a short video of their desperation.

Wow. Are you sure you don't want to try with one of them? That one who keeps trying to lift her shirt like it's Mardis Gras seems fun.

I'll stick with what I have, thank you very much. Wish you were here.

I'm having my own crazy person party of one. It's a blast! My mom is one step away from removing all the scissors from my room and replacing them with rounded safety scissors.

Doesn't she know you at all? Scissors are SO not your style.

I know, right??

"Hey, abandoned lovebird, your sister is about to sing," Parker said, nudging me. Sure enough when I looked up, Lottie was center stage now. The other two guys were apparently taking a break, even though they'd been playing one instrument to her three. It was just Lottie and her guitar and the microphone now as her band mates sat and mingled with their groupies.

Lottie started to play and sing and you could hear a pin drop. It was as if everyone immediately realized this girl was a caliber above everyone else they'd ever heard, as if she had that X-factor star quality that only came around once in a lifetime. Even if she hadn't been my sister, I could safely say she was the best I'd ever heard. She had that indefinable something her band members lacked. And they knew it, too, if the looks of resentment they shot her were any indication.

Parker noticed, too. "We might have to beat those guys up later," he whispered, clapping loudly as Lottie finished her song.

"I can't hit someone unprovoked," I said, but my fist flexed in anticipation. I didn't relish physical violence, I wasn't psychotic. But neither did I relish anyone disrespecting or disregarding my sister, as these guys were clearly doing. It was obvious they wanted to be the stars of the show and disliked Lottie because she was. The irony was that Lottie didn't want to be the star. She merely wanted to play, to be a part of making and performing music. She was humble about her gifts, an unassuming team player.

They must have caught the glares Parker and I were giving them because they smoothed their expressions as they took the stage. "Lottie Mulligan, everyone," one of them managed to say, motioning to her as a raucous burst of applause took over the room. A few people whistled. By a few people, I of course meant Parker and me.

Lottie returned to our table, cheeks flushed. "Usually it's just Mom or Dad at these things."

I felt another pinprick of conscience. Why hadn't I made more effort to attend? Our family was so large and so busy that Mom and Dad couldn't even usually go at the same time. While Haven and I had each other, Lottie had been left to float free, to find piecemeal time from everyone. Parker must have been feeling some sort of latent guilt, too, though I couldn't guess why. He hugged her in a tight squeeze.

"We're your new number one fans."

Lottie blushed under his praise, giggling like the fifteen year old she was.

"What's up with the morons?" Parker let her go and motioned to her band mates, now back among their adoring females. "Do we need to pound them or what?"

"Nah, they're not worth it," she said.

"Why don't you play with better people?" I asked.

She laughed, albeit humorlessly. "Who? Not to toot my own horn here, but no one is in my caliber. These are the only people I could find."

"Toot your own horn," Parker said, knocking his fist gently against her chin. "You Mulligans are so adorable."

Lottie batted his hand away and smoothed her hair. We listened to the next band a few minutes and decided to go. Lottie didn't say goodbye to the guys she'd played with, and they said nothing to her.

"Do they walk you out when we're not here?" I asked.

"No," she said, laughing.

I looked around the deserted street. "You can't ever come here alone."

"Okay, Dad," she said.

"I'm serious, Lottie. It's not safe for a girl to be walking around like this, this late at night. Someone needs to come with you when you start driving on your own."

"Who?" Lottie asked, a little sadly. "You'll be gone. Joel and Jonah are…"

"Joel and Jonah," I said. Our older brothers lived in a world of their own making, one where they were the stars of their weird universe. People thought I was odd because of the weather thing and the bees, but I had nothing on them. Much like Haven and me they'd always had each other. Somehow that had fed into their weirdness, making them an echo chamber for all their worst ideas.

"Exactly. The littles are too little and Mom and Dad are sometimes too busy."

"We'll figure it out," I assured her. "Maybe we'll tap Parker. He'll still be here next year." Parker was halfheartedly and aimlessly taking classes at the local community college with no plans to do anything else the next few years.

"Parker has the studly protective vibe down, as long as he's paying attention. But every time something shiny comes along, he drifts away," Lottie said.

"I can't argue with that," I agreed. I opened the door for her and closed it when she was safely inside. She let out a huge sigh as I buckled my safety belt.

"Why is it so hard to find someone? A person who wants to be your person, who gets you?"

"Because…" I began and stopped, suddenly out of answers.

"Because," Lottie repeated, tone subdued, as if the word held some meaning besides the obvious.

We were quiet until we pulled into the driveway, and then she spoke again. "Huntley?"

"Hmm."

"Growing up isn't turning out to be as much fun as I'd thought it would be."

I gave her what I hoped was a reassuring smile. "Stuff happens, Lottie. But you'll always have us, and your friends."

Her answering smile looked a little sad. "I don't really have any of those. I don't seem to fit anywhere."

"You fit with me, and I promise to do a better job of being there for you. I'm sorry I wasn't before. It wasn't on purpose. You and me, we're pals." I held up my fist, and she bumped it.

"You might win the best brother award this year. Don't tell the others."

"They won't hear it from me," I promised. Feeling lighter, we gathered her instruments and went inside.

CHAPTER 30

"I hate this place." Michelle sat in her usual position, chin tucked between her two hands, elbows on the table.

"I love this place," I said, staring at my phone, willing it to show a text from Bellamy. Three days. That was how long it had been since I heard from her. I was trying to give her space, but the waiting was unbearable.

"What do you love about it? The antiseptic-slash-urine smell, or the pall of human misery?" she asked.

"Ooh, pall. You don't hear that word often enough these days. Nice," I said, tucking my phone away as I pondered her question. "I guess what I love is that it's a place people go to get help. It seems definitive. Have a broken arm? Go to the hospital and get it fixed. Bam."

"I'd love to crack open your head, peep inside it like a little nut," she said, staring hard at me.

"I bet you would, you half-pint psycho." Over the last few days, we'd grown comfortable around each other, almost like we were becoming friends. *Proximity.* My unhelpful brain provided the word. I shooed it away, not wanting to think about why it bothered me in relation to Michelle, whose outer toughness was clearly a cover for a soft and gooey center.

"Why do you keep staring at your phone?" she asked.

"Nothing," I said, trying not to sigh.

"Girl trouble?" she guessed. "The clock is ticking on your inevitable breakup."

"Why inevitable?" I asked. "If two people want to be together, decide to be together, why can't they stay together?"

"Because life always finds a way to kick you in the teeth," Michelle said.

"Isn't that sort of the point of being together? So that when life kicks you in the teeth, you have a backup person to lean on?"

She had been reaching for a peanut from the open can between us. She paused, hand outstretched toward the nuts like a startled squirrel. "Maybe in fairytales of old. In real life people turn on each other, break under the stress, hurt each other even more, then one of them takes off, thereby abandoning the ashes of their relationship to the ruins." Her hand completed the journey, fingers tucking around two nuts before bringing them to her mouth.

"That's not always how it goes," I said, thinking of my parents.

She sighed, as if my great idiocy distressed her. "How can you believe in this junk? It's so naïve."

"No, it's a choice. Love is not some mystical, unknowable thing. It's a decision to show up and keep showing up, to put the other person above yourself, to do everything possible to bring them to a better version of themselves."

"Are you eighteen or eighty eight?" Michelle asked, but she sounded…wistful. We were silent a few beats. I was thinking about Bellamy and how my words applied to her. They were a confirmation of everything I already believed. Even if Bellamy was only my friend, sticking by her in the middle of this difficulty would have been the right thing to do. But we were more than friends. I had told her I loved her; that had to mean something more than words, didn't it? When did you give up on a person? My mom wanted me to give up now, before even helping Bellamy work through her emotional crisis.

That didn't feel right, but what if my mom knew more than I did? What if she understood something I hadn't yet discerned? Or was it only fear of putting me in harm's way that made her say the things she'd said?

Michelle similarly seemed to be thinking deep thoughts as she licked the salt off a peanut and put it in a growing pile on the desk. At any other time the mouth germs would have repulsed me, but I was too far gone in my own stupor to comment on it.

"It's nice, what you say," she said at last, as if the admission was hard for her. "Not very romantic, though. If I'm being honest." She shrugged, swept the pile of licked peanuts into her palm, and deposited them into the trash.

"What could be more romantic than sticking by someone through thick and thin?" I asked.

"Uh, maybe actual romance," she said.

"What is it with girls and romance?" I demanded. "A guy says he loves you, shows up, sticks by you, and you say that's not romantic."

"It's *nice*, it's not *romantic*. Big difference."

"So you'd rather have a guy who says all the right things but doesn't follow through?"

"Of course not," she said, growing impatient. She noted the peanut dust on her palm and then blew it toward my face. "Ideally we want both, and why is that so bad? Why can't we have a dependable guy who also says and does romantic things? Why do girls have to settle? It's not fair." She wrapped both arms around her knees, tucking them against her chest.

I opened my mouth to argue, and froze.

"What happened, are you broken?" Michelle asked, eyeing me with more curiosity than concern.

"No, I think maybe I'm having an epiphany," I said.

"Do you need to go to the emergency room and have it looked at?" she asked, but I ignored her because suddenly I knew exactly what I needed to do. What I didn't know was if I could, because it would take giving up the best thing that had ever happened to me.

The contrast between our houses was growing starker. Despite the fact that we had over eight thousand square feet, we could never get a minute alone at my place, my mom made sure of it. Bellamy's house was a quarter the size of ours, and yet here we were, completely alone.

"This is an awesome fort," I told her. It was the same thing I told her youngest brother when he showed it to me and said I could use it. I had assumed we would be sharing it with all the other kids, part and parcel of living in a big family. But Brooke shooed everyone outside, giving us the fort—and maybe the entire house—to ourselves.

"It's pretty great," Bellamy agreed. We lay on our backs side by side, holding hands and staring up at the ceiling of the fort.

"Did we make these?" I asked. I strained to remember making forts with Bellamy, but my mind was blank.

"I can't remember," she said, sounding as frustrated as I did.

"Why is that? It was only a few years ago. Do we really forget being kids this fast?"

"Some things you think you'll never forget slip away before you realize, and some things you wish you could forget never go away," she said. She swallowed hard, looking haunted.

I rolled toward her and gave her a smile. "I've missed you."

She rolled toward me, giving me a smile I could tell was forced. "I've missed you, too. I have something for you."

"You do?" I asked, perking up. It was pretty easy to tell where my mind was because I earnestly thought she was talking about making out. In my defense it had been days since I last kissed her, practically an eternity. She presented me with a little paper bag and a knowing smile. Maybe my poker face needed some work after all.

"Made you something," she said.

The fort was too short to allow sitting upright. Instead I placed the bag on my chest, pulled out the contents, and held it over my face. A bee painting stared back at me, a perfect water color. "You made this?" I said, awed.

"No biggie," she said, shrugging one shoulder. "Homeschoolers gonna craft."

"This is amazing and perfect, I love it. Thank you."

"Preemptive dorm decoration," she explained.

"The best," I said, staring hard at the picture. "I love it, so much." She stared at me while I admired the picture. I tucked it back in the bag and faced her.

"You're breaking up with me," she said, tone more resigned than sad.

"Never ever," I told her. Unable to resist touching her any longer, I pushed some of the stray hairs off her forehead.

"Why does it feel like it?"

"Because you're super smart." I took a breath for courage, swiping my hand gently over her head a few more times. "You know me. You know how I get something in my head, believe it's correct, and can't dislodge it."

She gave me a little nod of assent.

"You told me you needed space. I believed my way was better."

"And now you don't?" she asked.

"I still do. I don't want to be away from you. Staying apart is the worst, possibly my least favorite thing."

Her eyes clouded with confusion. "I don't understand."

"I didn't listen to you, and for that I'm sorry. Disregarding your request to give you space wasn't respectful to you or your needs."

Her lashes fluttered. I'd surprised her, I could tell.

"I'm going to try to listen better, to what you're telling me you need, not what I think you need."

She lay back, staring at the ceiling of the fort. "Oh. So...so this *is* a goodbye?"

"Sort of. Consider that part one."

Her mouth tipped into a smile I interpreted as hopeful. She faced me again, eyes bright. I reached for her hand.

"I was wrong about something else."

Her smile tipped. "No way, not Hot Huntley Mulligan."

"It happens occasionally, and you're going to enjoy this one: you were right." I squeezed her hand.

"About what? Don't tell me you've become a bee joke convert."

"I've become a Bellamy Brown convert, and that's the thing."

"What's the thing?"

"You're the thing, or rather the person, my person. I changed my mind about proximity."

Now her lashes fluttered furiously. "What? Why?"

"Because I've had a lot of proximity with a lot of different girls. I had proximity with you for eighteen of them. And it wasn't until camp that a switch flipped. I've spent a lot of time wondering why that happened, and I finally realized why."

"Why?" she asked, voice low and tight with anticipation.

"You are not random. *We* are not random. You are not some girl I had a chance encounter with or happened into. You are *my* girl, made special for me, my boho girl who completes me in all the ways, and maybe makes me a little bit crazy, too." I touched her never-behaved hair again.

Now the eyes I loved were teary, but I was adept enough in the ways of girls to recognize that they were happy tears, not sad.

"I love that," she whispered hoarsely. "But I still don't understand."

"It's like this: I'm going to go away, and I'm going to trust that the same power that brought us together the first time will bring us together again."

"Like, 'If you love something set it free, if it was meant to be it will come back?'"

I nodded. Keeping my face composed was harder than I realized it would be. There was a part of me, the biggest part, if I'm being honest, that didn't want to do this. I wanted to keep doing exactly what I had been doing—to keep showing up, being there, offering support, saying the right words. But it wasn't working. I was losing her, I could tell. Her fear and trauma were bigger than my faithful devotion, at least for now. I needed to give her space and time to heal; I needed to find a way to prove to her that this could work, would work. This was the only thing I could think of, and what I told her was true; somewhere along the way I had started to believe in true love, in soul mates, in finding a person who was so perfect for you there could be no one else.

Bellamy bit her lip, looking tentative and a little afraid. I resisted the urge to reassure her because part of this process would be her finding her own reassurance. "How is it going to work, specifically? You'll go away and wait for me to call you to come back?"

I shook my head. "I'll go away and stay away until we find each other by chance. Serendipity."

"You're serious," she said.

I nodded. "Totally and completely. I believe in us."

She clutched my shirt. "What if it doesn't happen?"

"It will."

"Okay, and don't take this the wrong way, but how can I know you won't make it happen? Our families are best friends; we do everything together. It wouldn't take much imagination or contrivance to arrange a meeting."

"It has to be outside our families. Planned family events don't count."

She licked her lips, blinking. "What about your mom?"

"My mom will come around." I said it with more confidence than I felt. What if she didn't? Could I be with someone my mom didn't approve of? On the other hand, if she didn't approve of Bellamy, who could she possibly approve of?

Bellamy clutched my shirt in both hands, looking as desperate as I previously felt before I reached this decision.

"It's going to be okay, I promise," I said.

Her grip relaxed slightly and she found her smile. "A Mulligan always keeps his promises."

I had never been more thankful for my family or the careful training that made her statement true. "Especially this one, especially to you."

"Are we allowed to kiss goodbye?" she asked, easing closer.

I rested my hand on her hip. "I see no need to waste this amazing fort."

Before she could reply, I kissed her.

CHAPTER 31

As soon as I let myself in the door, my mom emerged from the kitchen, dishtowel clutched anxiously in her hands. The Brown-to-Mulligan pipeline was working overtime, apparently. Brooke must have called with the news that Bellamy and I were taking a break. I could tell Mom wanted to say something but didn't know what. Both of us were afraid it would be the wrong thing.

"Huntley," she began, but even her tone set me on edge. My hands gripped into fists.

"Huntley." This time my dad spoke. My mom and I both jumped and spun to look. My dad had that almost supernatural ability to lurk unobserved in the places we least noticed him. Did he know what was going on with me and Bellamy? With me and Mom? Apparently. I wasn't certain I had intended to be disrespectful when I spoke, but maybe so because now I felt guilty and flushed under my father's inspection.

"Yes?" I said, trying hard to keep my tone neutral.

"I'm planning to do some pheasant hunting in the morning. Why don't you come with me?"

My lashes fluttered, surprised. Usually my oldest brothers accompanied Dad on his hunting expeditions. I had gone, but usually I tagged along, my head in the clouds. Somehow I knew this time it would be just me and dad, and that it was important.

"Sounds good," I agreed.

Dad gave a nod and hovered, protectively, I thought. As if he needed to be the buffer between Mom and me. Maybe he did. All I knew was that I felt raw and wounded and not in the mood to hear her say anything negative about Bellamy or our imposed separation. With a nod of my own, I spun and went the other direction, meaning the basement. I was ready to escape to bed, but there was no way to go upstairs without skirting by my parents.

As I drew nearer the basement, I heard someone crying. With eight kids, it wasn't unusual for one of us to be crying, but this one sounded more wrenching than a skinned knee or sibling disagreement. This was the cry of utter heartbreak, and my heart wrenched in response, especially when I entered the room and saw Lottie weeping, her head tucked against...Parker?

Parker gave me such a caught, startled look that at first I thought he must be the source of the tears. But before I could mount up a defense, I realized the truth. Lottie was far too sensible to cling to someone who would hurt her so deeply. Parker must simply be shocked to be the go-to comforter for once. He patted Lottie's back, tossing me a helpless glance.

"Lottie, what's wrong?" I asked, perching hesitantly beside her. She shook her head. I turned to Parker for an explanation.

"They kicked her out of the band," he said, barely repressed ire in his tone.

"What?" I exclaimed, letting free all the rage Parker was trying to hide.

Lottie clutched at Parker's shirt, huddling further.

"You're the best part of that band, the very best part," I added in a softer tone, but that only made her cry harder because she already knew that. This wasn't a rejection of Lottie's skills, but rather of Lottie herself. Not being averse to the ways of girls, I realized that probably hurt more.

"I tried to explain to Lottie that her amazing and impressive skills and talent threatened them because it highlighted their complete lack of both," Parker said, giving Lottie an encouraging squeeze. "I think the lesson will sink in better after we beat the ever loving…"

Lottie reached up to press her hand to his mouth, muffling whatever word came next.

"Right," I agreed with a nod, and both of them yanked apart to stare at me. "What?"

"You'd beat someone up?" Parker said.

"For me?" Lottie added.

"I can't think of a better reason," I answered both of them. They both continued to stare at me, matching disbelieving expressions. "What?"

"You're so…Huntley," Parker said.

I didn't know why that annoyed me, but it did. "There's a time for peace, and a time for violence. Pretty sure the line separating the two is when someone hurts your little sister."

Lottie blinked and shook her head as if to clear it. "I don't want that."

"Why not?" Parker asked. The fact that he seemed ridiculously eager to fight gave me pause. If Parker was on board with something, it was a safe bet it was the wrong side.

"Because you guys are eighteen. You could get in trouble. You could get arrested," Lottie said, looking worried.

"Don't worry about it," Parker said, waving away her worry like so many gnats.

"No, I'm serious. I don't want you to hurt anyone. It will make everything worse," Lottie said.

"Lottie, this is man stuff," Parker declared, aiming for authoritative and failing greatly.

She rolled her eyes and focused on me. "Please, Huntley. It would make me feel worse. Please don't."

"If you don't want us to hit them, we won't. But we're going to have a conversation."

"What? No," Lottie said, still looking horrified and embarrassed.

I stood and put down a hand to help her up. "You can come if you want, but we'll go with or without you."

"I don't need my brother to fight my battles for me," she said, frowning at my hand.

"Yes, you do," I told her. "This is what brothers do, and Parker's right."

Parker's head snapped up. "I am? Not sure I've ever heard that before, especially from a Mulligan."

"This is guy stuff," I elaborated. "There's stuff going on here you don't understand, a level of misogyny that needs to be dealt with."

Lottie started to grin, tried to bite it back, and gave up. "Since you invoked the patriarchy, I guess I have to go along."

"Girl power," Parker agreed, unfurling himself from the floor.

I didn't disagree, but it had nothing to do with girl power and everything to do with guy power, and the misuse thereof. These boys thought they could push Lottie around because she was younger and unprotected and a girl; they were about to learn otherwise the hard way. Some people said needing a man for a protector was an outdated concept. I disagreed. I had seen too much of how the world regarded my sisters and Bellamy to leave them to their own devices. What girls needed was a *good* man on their side, someone who looked out for their best interests without trampling them in the process. I had no desire to keep them down or hold them back; on the contrary, I wanted them to grow and thrive. But I could also see there were other people in the world, sometimes men, who wanted the opposite. If I could be the one to stand in the gap and pave the way, making it smoother for them, so much the better.

If I were being even more honest with myself, there was a part of me that felt retroactive guilt that I hadn't done enough for Bellamy. I knew what camp she was talking about because I was supposed to go to it. Haven went every year and had begged me to tag along. I always refused because I was too afraid and anxious to try new things and be away from home, even if I would still be with Haven. If I had gone that year, would I have realized what was going on? Would I have understood that the counselor's interest in Bellamy was predatory?

Would I have intervened and protected her? Or, at the very least, told one of our parents what was going on?

I would never know because my fear held me back, fear of taking a step outside my comfort zone that caused me to stay home. How much more had my fear cost me? What if I hadn't gone to weather camp? I had been on the fence about it, wavering back and forth until a couple of days before, almost sick with anxiety over the thought of leaving home and everything familiar. It was only the desire to try and find closure about my future major that had finally driven me to go. And look what I'd gained, not only a major, but Bellamy. It felt like my future had been decided in all the best possible ways, and all because I took a leap. I vowed to keep taking them, to not let the fear and anxiety drag me back again and stop me from living.

Now I opened the back door for Lottie, waiting to close it until she was safely inside, turning away from the car to hide my smile. Lottie's demeanor had changed from morose to almost excited. I hated to see her sad and hurt; bloodthirsty was a better option.

Parker was similarly enthused. He sat in the front seat like a golden retriever on its way to the park, drumming his hands on the dash and humming a tune only he knew.

"I'll be your new band mate, Lottie," he said.

Lottie cringed. "Wow, that's…quite the offer, Parker. Maybe you can be my road crew."

"What?" he said, aghast with mock affront. "I am so much more than a roadie. Have you seen my face?" Here he pointed to himself.

"Yeah, I've seen your face," she said, leaning forward to give his cheek an affectionate pat. He winked at her and smiled, she sat back and smiled, staring out her window in silence.

We were all quiet as I drove to the place where the guys hung out, also the place where Lottie had band practice. It was basically someone's garage, and I once again wondered at the wisdom of letting her go places like this alone. Not for the first time I felt like maybe Lottie had been swept to the side and ignored in our large family, left to fend for herself and try to find her own way. Once again I vowed to do better, to pay more attention and spend time with her.

I parked and studied the house, trying to figure out how much I wanted to punch these guys. I was about at a five on the ten scale. Parker seemed more eager, possibly a seven, but by now I knew him well enough to feel confident that he would follow my lead. *My lead.* The thought startled me because I was usually never the one in the lead, until now. I pushed that away for later, getting myself back into the moment, and turned to Lottie. "Are you coming or staying in the car?"

She bit her lip as she regarded the house, looking apprehensive. "Staying here." It came out like a shaky question.

I reached behind the seat and gave her knee a reassuring squeeze. "Probably for the best."

"Man stuff," Parker affirmed, squeezing her other knee.

She gave us a tremulous smile and clutched her hands together. "Wish I'd brought something to play," she muttered. While other kids might be referring to a phone or game, Lottie meant one of her instruments—mandolin, ukulele, guitar. If it had strings, it was pretty much guaranteed she could play it.

"We'll be quick," I promised and got out of the car.

Parker got out on his side and we walked side by side to the house. I knocked a few times, hard enough to sting my knuckles.

"Power knock," Parker said, nodding his approval. "Good start."

One of the guys opened the door and I realized I didn't know his name. Travis, maybe? Travyn? Travers? *A good brother would know his sister's bandmates,* I thought, chastising myself for my lack.

"Can we come in?" I asked.

"Yeah?" the guy said, but it sounded like a question. Regardless, he moved aside, watching us as we trooped in. I stared around the space, dark and dank and reeking of must and BO. A sad looking drum set was in the corner, along with a couple of guitars, an amp, and a disgusting orange couch that, if the stains were any indication, had seen things I never wanted to know about. *My little sister has been coming here every night, exposed to these creeps who could have done absolutely anything to her at any point.* I took a deep breath, thinking of Bellamy and feeling sick.

Anything could have happened to Lottie, anything at all, and where had I been?

"So," I said. My hands automatically curled into fists. I crossed my arms over my chest. Parker did the same, looking macho and annoyed.

"So…" the guy said, once again making it a question with his tone.

"I think you owe my sister an apology," I said.

He flinched and paled. "Who's your sister?"

"Lottie," Parker growled.

The guy blinked at us, looking confused. "Why would I owe Lottie an apology? I never touched her. Not like I would."

"What's wrong with Lottie?" Parker demanded, getting sidetracked from our original outrage. If these guys weren't attracted to Lottie, it was good news, as far as I was concerned.

"She's kind of a freak," the guy said.

"Define freak," I said, anger barely controlled.

"I don't know, weird and only into the music."

We blinked at him. "You're a band."

"Yeah, but it's about more than the music, you know? It's about the vibe, the group."

"Lottie is amazing," Parker said.

The guy quirked an eyebrow at him. "I mean, she's got some talent, but we could never gel with her."

"Because she's ten thousand times better than you and you stink?" I guessed.

"No, because she weighed us down, made it all weird and stilted. Like trying to make your cat lady aunt a member of the band. Girl's a frea…" he didn't get to finish because Parker punched him in the face. The guy dropped like a badly constructed high rise, and clutched his face. His yelp worked to summon his friend from the kitchen. He came in drinking beer from a can, using a paper straw.

"A straw, really?" Parker said.

The guy looked at his friend, looked at us, and took a sip.

"You owe my sister an apology," I began.

"Which one is your sister?" he said.

Parker sighed. "This again. Geez, these guys are morons."

"They really are," I agreed. "Much more than I realized. Lottie, my sister is Lottie, although I'm rethinking the apology because you did her a massive favor by kicking her out of your band. So let's revise: when you inevitably realize that Lottie was the only reason anyone on earth wanted to hear you play or book you for anything, don't call her. Don't come near, don't contact her. In fact, if you see her walking down the street, cross to the opposite side so you won't breathe the same air as her. Are we clear?"

The guy who was still standing scratched his head. "I guess, okay. Yeah."

I turned to Parker. "Did you want to hit this one?"

"Seems cruel and unfair to his remaining brain cell," Parker said. He toed the guy on the ground, but gently. We turned and walked outside, taking a deep breath of the cool, fresh night air.

"Feels weird to be the good guy for once," Parker mused.

"You could always be the good guy," I told him. "The world needs more."

"Sometimes being bad feels good," Parker returned.

"I guess you need to try to find a way to be bad for a good reason," I said.

Parker slung his arm around my shoulders. "Huntley, you're kind of brilliant, you know that?"

Lottie leaned forward anxiously, poking her head between our seats. "What happened?"

"They wept and begged to have you back. We said you're unavailable," Parker told her.

"You're lying," Lottie said, but she was smiling.

Parker gave me a nod, and I knew what he was thinking. *Bad for a good reason.* I smiled, too, feeling pretty light for a guy who had no idea when he would ever see his girlfriend again.

CHAPTER 32

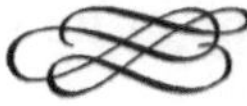

Hunting with my dad meant an early morning. I was an early riser naturally, but still had to set my alarm for our four AM wakeup.

Dad and I were silent as we loaded his truck and drove. Our bird dog, Jetta, darted its head between us, panting happily. The dog was actually Joel's. My brothers were into all things country, including guns, dogs, and trucks. You'd think we lived off the grid somewhere instead of in a mansion at the edge of town.

Even though I was tense and expectant over our coming conversation, the early morning with dad was peaceful and appreciative. He was the head of a giant company, and he had eight kids. Having him all to myself was an unexpected treat.

He waited to speak until we'd walked a few paces, the overgrown brush skimming our calves. I tensed, but what he said was so surprising I let out a puff of air in exclamation.

"Have you ever noticed that your mom doesn't smile using her teeth?"

I blinked, trying to picture my mom's smile, a weird thing to do in the early dawn stillness. "Why? Mom has a beautiful smile."

Now Dad smiled. "The most beautiful smile in the world. When she was fourteen she got a tooth infection so bad she almost died. That was the first time she went to the dentist in her life. You know Mom's early life was riddled with chaos and neglect, and that was not without consequence. So many years of poor nutrition and neglect combined into the perfect storm. She had to have a couple of teeth pulled, things weren't where they were supposed to be, there was a lot of rotting and decay. It was a mess, and so painful and traumatic. They couldn't afford to knock her out, so they had to go with the cheap and non-working anesthesia. She felt most of it. For years she was terrified of the dentist. After Margaret was born, she powered through her fear and got veneers. She waited all that time because she didn't want to do anything while she was pregnant or nursing that might harm one of you kids, but it was a constant insecurity for her."

I thought back to my childhood and our twice-yearly dental checkups. To my knowledge, we'd never missed one, and Mom's hyper anxiety about getting us there began to make sense.

"Poor nutrition?" I said, capturing on the other part of the sentence that didn't make sense. Nutrition was my mom's life. She was always stuffing us with something healthy, monitoring our junk food intake like a strict prison warden.

"One day in high school your mom overheard the school nurse saying some of the people in the Irish Potato Famine probably had better nutrition than some of the kids they dealt with because she'd watched a kid eat a bag of Skittles as her lunch. That kid was your mom. She was mortified, and that was the first inkling she had that she wasn't eating properly. She got a book on nutrition from the library and realized how many of her chronic health problems were caused by the food she and her family ate." He paused as I pictured my mom as a teenager, checking out books from the library to try and fix her health. "Did you know it was your mom's idea to buy the car wash?"

I blinked at him in surprise. In our family, Dad worked and Mom managed the house. I assumed that was how it had always been. This was my first indication that Mom had any input on the business. "Really?"

He nodded, his smile amused and self-deprecating. "We both knew we wanted to give our kids a better life than we had, but we were eighteen with no skills, barely a high school degree between us. Then your mom thought how, no matter what was going on in life, her grandpa would scrape together enough change to wash the car. He said it was better to pay a little for a wash than a lot for rust, after all the road salt. She thought if her family was willing to pay for a car wash, poor as they were, probably a lot of other people would be, too. But of course no one would give two dumb kids a loan, especially with no credit. So we got jobs working fast food full time." Now his smile turned wry. "But your mom wouldn't let us eat any of the food, by that time. We were probably the only people working there who wouldn't eat our product."

I laughed because *that* sounded like the mom I knew.

"We lived in a dump, walked everywhere we needed to go so we wouldn't have to pay for a car or insurance or gas, and put every spare penny into our savings. I mean every penny. We had no Christmases, birthdays, or vacations. We bought nothing but the absolute necessities. By nineteen we were both managing our restaurants, which gave us a much needed boost in income. After three years of saving every penny, we had enough to buy the first wash."

"And the rest is history," I said.

He shook his head. "Not quite. It started to draw a profit right away, and I, dummy I was, was content with that. I thought we were rich, was practically ready to retire. Your mom had other ideas. She wouldn't let us keep that money, made us keep working our other jobs while we put the profits from the wash into two more washes. Then five more. By the time Jonah was born, we owned ten washes, and only *then* did she quit her job and let us draw an income off our investment." He glanced at me. "Your mom's a business tycoon, a boot strapper, the most cunning and driven woman I've ever met. She works harder than anyone I've ever known, powers through every drop of exhaustion. But not without a price." He paused. "There are other scars from her childhood besides her teeth, hidden things you don't see. She tries so hard to keep going, to not let stuff bother her.

One of her coping mechanisms is to hyper manage everything, the meticulous house, the laborious meals, homeschooling, everybody's sports and music lessons. She so desperately wants you kids to have a better life than she had. When the thing with Bellamy came up…" He paused, and I tensed. "It was something outside her control. That was really hard for her."

I paused and faced him, also choosing my words, a battle because I wanted to yell and rant about the unfairness of everything, the pressure Mom had added to our relationship, the hurt she'd heaped on Bellamy, who didn't deserve it. Instead what I said was, "It's been hard for me, too."

Dad stopped walking and faced me, his expression grave and intent. I prepped myself for a lecture. Instead what he said was, "I know. And I'm really proud of you."

I blinked, sifting the words for hidden meaning, but I couldn't seem to find any. "Pardon?"

"I've watched you with your mom, with Bellamy, with Lottie. You've really stepped up, Huntley. You've become a leader. You've kept your temper in check with your mom and treated her with respect, even when your feelings told you not to. You haven't wallowed in your hurt over Haven, closeting yourself away with your hobbies. Instead you've reached out to Lottie, to take care of her and try to ease some of her loneliness. The maturity and growth I've witnessed in you these last few months makes me so proud. It makes me believe you are worthy of all the trust and freedom we've given you, probably more. Good job." He reached out and gave my shoulder a firm squeeze.

Now I blinked furiously, trying to tamp down my tears, feeling shamed over all the times I hadn't felt quite so mature or magnanimous, over all the times I wanted to yell at Mom or closet myself away from Lottie and her needs, or run and hide instead of step up and lead. In short I felt a raw mix of gratified and unworthy. "What do I do about Mom?"

Dad shrugged. "Nothing. Mom will get there when she gets there. Believe me when I tell you, after two and a half decades of marriage, that nothing will make her get there faster. Just keep being a good son, being a good *man*."

We faced forward again and started to walk. The dog darted into the brush and flushed out a pheasant who took flight, majestically, I thought. My dad gave me a nudge. "You take this one."

I shouldered my gun, took a breath, and lowered the weapon. "Dad."

"Hmm."

"I hate hunting. I mean, I like coming out here and walking around with you, but I hate shooting the birds. They're so beautiful. And field dressing triggers my gag reflex."

To my further surprise, Dad laughed. "Me, too. Let's let the dog get some exercise and tell your brothers it was a wash, deal?"

"Deal," I said, feeling lighter than I had in a long, long time.

When we arrived home, Mom had fresh whole grain muffins for us, sweetened with maple syrup, of course. Her smile was apprehensive, and now I saw what I never had before, the way her lips worked hard to cover all her teeth. I thought about what Dad said, and then I thought about Bellamy. If this was her, how would I want someone to react, knowing she was still dealing with so much pain? So I did what I hadn't done since I got home from camp—I hugged my mom. Hard, an all-in Mulligan sort of hug that left her no option but to hug me hard in return. She did so and broke on a sob, even though her eyes were dry when she pulled away.

"Thanks for the muffins," I said, reaching for one, but I meant something else. *Thanks for working so hard to get your life together, thanks for taking care of me and everyone else, thanks for being my mom, even when we disagree.*

"You're welcome," she said, giving me an eagle-eyed stare that made me wonder if she was saying something else, too.

CHAPTER 33

The night Parker and I went after Lottie's band mates, we inadvertently became her new road crew. And somehow we became a trio, always together when we weren't at work or in school. Lottie was still searching for a new band, but in the meantime she began to book some venues solo, and it was…nice. Unexpectedly nice, for someone who was missing his girlfriend like a hole in his chest. As the days slid into weeks, I didn't miss Bellamy any less. Instead it became a constant ache, an echo, a constant battle to keep the fear and anxiety at bay. What if…

But that was where I always stopped myself. I wouldn't let doubt gain a foothold. This was the right thing to do; Bellamy and I would find our way back to each other, I had to believe that. Otherwise what was the point of everything?

But what if…

"Earth to Huntley," Lottie said, and I realized we'd reached our destination. She'd kept it a surprise, but now that I tuned in and realized where we were, I sat up in alarm.

"Lottie," I exclaimed, turning to face her over the console. She was within days of getting her license, and she was doing a great job with driving, so great that I often zoned out when I was her passenger.

Today that had been to my undoing because we were somewhere we definitely shouldn't be.

"What? I'm taking you for pancakes," Lottie said, aiming for innocence and failing greatly.

"I can't go here," I said, pointing to the building.

"Why not?"

"Because this is where Bellamy works as a waitress," I said.

"Is it?" she asked, trying and failing feigned innocence again.

"You know it is, and you know it doesn't count if our meeting was arranged by our families."

She put up her hands in mock surrender. "Look, I just want to take my big brother out for a nice meal, to thank him for all he's done to help me with my career lately. Can I help it if I coincidentally picked the place where his long-lost girlfriend might currently be working?"

I knew her argument was ridiculous, but the tempting pull of Bellamy was too great. I hadn't seen her in months, hadn't held her, kissed her, not even glimpsed her, and I missed her so much, it was like a part of my body had stopped functioning. "Okay," I said, and Lottie beamed. "Don't gloat," I warned, darting a finger at her. She wiped her expression and aimed for a solemn nod, something that looked totally wrong on her face. My sister was sort of ornery rotten, I had come to realize. Also, I totally loved that about her. Whenever shenanigans were afoot, Lottie was there for them. It was a shame that fewer people realized how awesome she was, but I was also certain her day would come, when more people would catch on to the fact that Lottie Mulligan was amazing, in all the ways.

My heart thumped wildly as we pushed open the door of the café, the smell of stale coffee and old grease smacking us in the face. Despite my eagerness to see Bellamy, it was not a pleasant smell, and I felt bad she had to stew in it all day long. I wondered, not for the first time, how she was doing, how she could possibly be doing better when this was where she had to work everyday, when she had so much on her plate, to try and deal with it alone. What if…

No, I wouldn't allow myself to go there, to go anywhere. And this meeting wouldn't count. I would merely say hi, reassure myself she was okay, and resume our no-contact rule.

But it turned out to be a moot point. As soon as we entered and saw Parker waiting for us in the booth, he relayed the bad news. "Sorry, Dude, it's not her shift. A few other hot waitresses, though. I got numbers."

"Wait a minute," Lottie said, squinting suspiciously at him. She and I slid into the same side of the booth, which meant Parker was opposite us. "Are you trying to tell me there are still girls in this town you haven't gone out with?"

"Only the younger and older demographic," Parker said, with a full cocky gloat that made Lottie gag.

He picked up her hand and held it between both of his. "Don't be jelly, babe. You know you're my number one girl."

"Aw, Parker, that's like being told I'm the number one unwanted dog at the no-kill shelter," Lottie said.

"You're welcome," Parker said sincerely, kissing her hand.

I studied them closely, once again making certain I wasn't missing something between them. Haven was the one who was good at picking up on nonverbal clues. I generally had to be hit over the head to see things like that. But, try as I might, I didn't sense any hints of romance between Parker and Lottie, despite their close friendship. It was more like they were becoming each other's missing piece, and I was glad. They would both need someone next year when I was gone, someone to look out for the other, to pay attention, to take care of the other. It was nice that they had each other. More than nice, I realized as I stared into space, thinking. It was *serendipitous.* That Parker and Lottie, who were a few years apart in age, galaxies apart in experience and popularity, should have been brought together to become not only friends, but close friends, the way they now were, could only be by design, by purpose.

"I think we broke your brother," Parker said, Lottie's hand still clasped between both of his. "He's staring dreamily into space. Is he thinking of bees?"

"Huntley," Lottie said softly, reaching out a free hand to touch my forearm. "You doing okay over there?"

"Yes," I croaked, drawing myself out of my daydreams, because I really was okay. "Everything is going to be all right. It will all work out." My voice was fused with more assurance than I'd used in weeks, if not months. I swallowed hard and nodded my head, gaining momentum on my certainty.

"Uh-huh," Parker agreed, nodding exaggeratedly. "Did the bees tell you it was going to be okay? Do they appear to you often?"

I gave his hand a shove, knocking it away from Lottie's. "Buzz off, or I'm withdrawing my sister for your consideration."

"You Mulligans are so cute, with your empty threats and righteous indignation," Parker said, resting his chin in his fists as he gazed adoringly at us.

"Parker, why do you keep saying 'you Mulligans' when you're clearly one of us now?" Lottie asked, and Parker's lashes fluttered, taken aback by the invitation into our family dynamic.

"True story," I said, leaning forward. "You've been Mulligan adjacent for too long. You now have Mulligan DNA."

"You're going to be a good doctor," Parker said to me, but his cheeks were endearingly pink. Parker was so good at blowing smoke and working his charm that it was always good to see him a little off kilter.

"That's right, I am. Now let's pound some bacon and pancakes with fake syrup and margarine before Mom's beacon goes off and she swoops in to force feed us bone broth and kale," I said, reaching for a menu.

While we ate, we talked. Or rather Lottie and Parker talked and plotted, about ways to get me and Bellamy together. As the meal went on, their plotting became more bizarre and far-fetched.

"Yes, but how will we get them both on a mission to Mars?" Parker asked at one point.

"It's so simple, I can't believe I have to go over this again," Lottie said, and then went on to explain in such a way that had us doubled over in laughter.

I had another one of those moments where I took a step back and looked at my life, like viewing it through someone else's lens. Haven and Sutton were at college. Bellamy was wherever Bellamy was. I was in a weird in-between, not in high school, not in college, and yet everything was absolutely and one hundred percent okay. Better than okay, it was pretty amazing. Wherever Bellamy was, I hoped she was surrounded by love and laughter and friendship and family, the way I was. I hoped she was finding not just healing, but joy and laughter. And somehow, wrapped in my newfound love of serendipity, I believed maybe she was. Because the only thing that would make it right enough for us to come back together would be for her to be healed and whole enough to finally be in a relationship. I would need to trust this time apart, to trust that God had a plan for both of us, not just me.

"But what do the bananas have to do with it?" Parker asked, wiping tears of laughter from his eyes.

"Only everything," Lottie exclaimed, tossing her hands wide. Parker doubled over laughing again, and I felt like my heart grew twelve times, overflowing with love for everything and everyone.

This, I thought. *No matter where I go, no matter what's going on, I want more of these perfect moments.* It was enough to find a minute of laughter with my friends; really, it was everything.

CHAPTER 34

"You are going to get on that," I said, pointing as the tiny train made its way around the tiny track.

Michelle stared at the train, then turned to stare at me. She opened her mouth, and I smashed my palm over it, stopping the regrettable word before it could leave her mouth. After so many outings together, I could tell already what it was going to be. And instead of speaking, she grinned against my palm, waiting to speak until I dropped my hand. "Thanks, I needed that. But also, no way, no how am I riding that train."

I tipped my head, studying her. "Have you ever ridden a train before?"

She shook her head.

I pointed to the train.

"Huntley, that is not a train. It's barely even a ride. It's a sad old man's hobby, turned into a cash cow." We both surveyed the eager line of parents, queued up with money in hand so their little darlings could take a turn on the train.

"What is the point of being here, if not to gain new experiences for you?" I asked.

"Exactly," she said, tossing her hands wide in angry exasperation. "What is the point of being here?"

A few weeks ago Michelle and I had started taking outings together. I hesitated to call them dates, because they weren't. At first I thought she'd had a little crush on me and after a bit of stilted—and angry—awkwardness on her part, she tried to kiss me. I gently rebuffed her with the explanation that she didn't actually like me, she liked what I represented—stability and security, both things she had never had before. As I'd first suspected, Michelle worked at the hospital as a condition of her probation. Her family was MIA, and she'd predictably gotten into trouble. Over the last few weeks I'd made it my mission to try and re-parent her, to give her new experiences she'd never had before, in order to offer her a sort of do over. After I'd explained to her that her feelings for me were not romantic, because she didn't understand familial love, she had stared at me in confusion, the hard set of her features softening into something like affection.

"You're so weird," she mused.

And that was that. We were not dating, but we were taking weekly outings together. The problem, we quickly realized, was that we had absolutely nothing in common. Nothing that interested me—minerals, bees, the weather, all things science and medicine—interested her in the slightest. And the things that interested her—death metal, tattoos, and gross art exhibits—scared me greatly. We compromised by opening the newspaper at the hospital to the events section, closing our eyes, and jabbing a finger at random. Wherever the finger landed, that was where we went or what we did. So far we'd gone to an auction together, where I bought an awesome vintage globe. Michelle made fun of me, until I presented the globe to her, in order to show her there was more to the world than she currently knew. Then she got kind of teary and slugged me hard in the arm, so I thought she kind of liked it.

Next we went to a horse show and, surprisingly, Michelle liked that more than I did. She was enamored by all the varieties of horses. Maybe it was a girl thing; my sisters liked horses, too. I didn't really see the appeal. A horse was a horse. What did it matter if you braided their tails?

We went to bingo at the Catholic Church and both enjoyed it so much we'd gone back three times, bringing the median age down to about ninety. The old people loved to see us there and, though Michelle would never admit it, I think brightening their day brightened hers, too. I was trying to teach her that doing things for others was a surefire way to do something for yourself, but she met my proclamations with a scowl and no comment, so I wasn't certain I was having an effect. Yet. I had a few weeks left before school, plenty of time to make a dent in her badly broken armor.

"You're doing it," I said now, fishing for my wallet.

Michelle huffed a sigh, but didn't argue. That told me she actually wanted to ride the ride, but was too embarrassed to admit it, which was what I'd suspected all along when her eyes glommed onto the ride as soon as we stepped into the door.

We waited in line, I paid the man, then stood on the sidelines to take pictures. If the ride had been able to hold me, I would gladly have ridden with her. But I was over six feet tall, much too big for the tiny ride, as the guy told me unbidden when I paid for Michelle. I contented to stand on the sidelines and take pictures like a proud parent while Michelle made the circle, her arms crossed over her chest in mutinous surrender.

I took a step back, to try to get a better angle, and mashed into someone, whirling as I made my apology. "I'm so sorry," I said as she said the same thing.

Then we stopped short and stared at each other, mouths agape.

Bellamy stared up at me, cheeks pink and hair askew from the cool and windy spring day. "Are you real?" she whispered.

I nodded, grinning, and then my smile slipped. "Did Lottie call you, trick you into being here?"

She shook her head. "Our car broke down with a flat tire."

Now my eyes narrowed for certain. "Who is we?"

"Me and Dylan."

My scowl turned thunderous. "Are you on a date?"

She put her hands on her hips, temper flaring in pure Bellamy fashion. "Excuse me, I have a boyfriend. *In absentia.*"

I grinned like the love-addled fool I was. "Are you actually telling me this guy doesn't know how to change a tire?"

She shook her head, smile quirking so her dimple flashed. My heart stopped and turned over. The ride must have stopped because suddenly Michelle was beside me, and now Bellamy was the one flaring with undue jealousy. Before I could remedy the situation, Michelle came to the rescue. "I'm Michelle, Huntley's quasi-adopted daughter. Are you my new mommy?"

"She's been your mommy all along," I told her, turning back to Bellamy. "*In absentia.*"

The missing Dylan sidled up to us then, and I'm not going to lie—I was shallow enough to appreciate the several inches I had over him. He glanced at me and then at Michelle, who gave him a once over in return.

"You're sort of hot, in a dork kind of way. Want to go somewhere and make out, give the lovebirds some privacy?" She held out her hand to him, not giving him another option, not that he looked too sad to take it and tag along behind her. She was pretty, in a scary goth chick sort of way.

"I'm going to assume you'll explain all that later," Bellamy said. "Is he safe with her?"

"I don't know. A guy who can't change a tire may not be safe anywhere," I said, smiling when she snorted an adorable laugh. Unable to resist any longer, I reached out and pushed her hair away from her face. "Hey, I missed you. Also, I love you. How are you?"

She bit her lip and clutched my shirt in her fists, tipping closer. "I'm actually…kind of incredible. How about you?"

"Shooting laser beams of love, all over the place."

She nodded her agreement. "I feel like someone popped open my head and shoved a candle inside, like I'm actually glowing. And also, I wanted to tell you that you were right."

"About what?" I asked. I tried hard to listen, but it was difficult not to stare at her lips and tune everything else out, except how much I wanted to kiss her.

"About everything, which is super annoying for a person like me, who prides herself on being right all the time. But I did need this break, I needed you to go away so I could heal."

"And did you? Heal?"

"I did my best," she said. She took a breath, gearing up, then let it out in a rush. "I went to see him."

I froze. "*Him?*"

She nodded. "My mom took me, actually, when she realized how much I needed it. I confronted him in the street and read him a letter I'd written about how much he harmed me, how much he stole from me."

"What did he say? What did he do?"

"Nothing. He stood there and stared at me, eyes wide, lips silent. I think maybe he was afraid I was wearing a wire or something and anything he said could be used against him in a court of law."

"Or maybe he's a cowardly weasel."

"Well, there's that. Because what I realized, when I saw him again after so much time, was that I had built him up too much in my head. I made him larger than life—suaver, handsomer, eviler. In reality he's some guy, more pathetic than most, maybe. And I had another epiphany while I was there. Maybe more than one." She huffed another breath. "First of all, I told him I forgive him. I hadn't written that part, because I surely didn't feel it. But as I was standing there reading his list of sins, I realized they only continued to hurt me because I let them, and I don't want to let them anymore. I don't want to be a victim; I want to be an overcomer. So I said the words, 'I forgive you.'"

"What happened then?" I asked.

"Nothing. Mom and I left and got something to eat. I expected to have a breakdown or feel some monumental shift. Instead I felt a tiny bit lighter, maybe two percent. And then the next morning when I woke up, I repeated the words. 'I forgive him, and I'm letting this go.' And I kept repeating them every morning until I didn't have to say them anymore, until I *felt* them. And then the real healing and lightness began. Everything kept going up and up and up, which was sort of miraculous because I was still under the same load—still taking the same classes and working the same hours and you were gone. But *I* was different. I felt so good, so strong, like I could handle anything."

"You can," I inserted vehemently.

"I know," she said, dashing her hands wide with Bellamy enthusiasm that made me laugh. "And, Huntley," she clasped my shirt in her fists again, giving it a little shake. "I love you so much. That never wavered, not once. I never had a second of doubt about you, about us."

"Me neither," I said. I brushed my hand on her neck, noting her reaction with pleasure when she shivered and leaned into my touch. She closed her eyes and tipped forward, and then her eyes popped open and she reeled back.

"Oh, no, I just remembered."

"What?"

"College."

"You just remembered college?" I said, amused.

She shook her head. "I just remembered we're supposed to go to college, and we won't be together. We've been apart so long, and now we're only going to be together a few months and have to part again." Her pretty eyes filled with tears that she tried valiantly to blink away.

I shook my head. "It's not a problem."

"Because of serendipity?" she asked.

"No, because we're going to college together."

Her eyes narrowed in confusion. "Huh?"

"You told me to pick our college, so I picked," I said, shrugging.

"But it's too late for me to apply to wherever you picked," she said.

I rolled my eyes. "Bellamy, come on, have a little faith in the Mulligan system. Obviously I already applied for you."

Now her blinks turned slow and confused. "What?"

I glowed with the accomplishment of having achieved my goal and kept it secret. "I applied to my top three colleges, and so did you."

"But...how?"

"My mom helped me. She got all your information from Brooke. It felt a little too much like cheating to write your essays, so I had Lottie do it. The good news is she's brilliant and you got accepted to all three. The bad news is that if anyone ever mentions your essays, you're going to have to bluff your way through a lot of music similes and references."

She swallowed hard, pupils dilating with shock. "Your...mom... helped...you?"

I nodded, making a soothing pass over her hair again. "Mom is sorry for before. She apologized to me, and she's gotten fully on board with you, with us. Look I have proof." I removed a wadded piece of material from my pocket and shoved it at her. She held it up, staring at it in wonder.

"It's my monogram," she said, awed.

"It's your future monogram, for after you become a Mulligan. Mom's been practicing on her sewing machine so she can put it on all of our presents."

"Your mom believes in us enough to make us monogram official?" she whispered, tears shimmering on her lashes again.

I nodded.

"It doesn't get any more official than that," she said, dashing at her eyes before they made their way back to me. "You've been carrying this around, waiting to run into me?"

I nodded.

"Huntley," she said.

"Yes?"

The grin spread over her face as she spoke. "Why didn't the insect want to work out?"

"No. Stop it. I beg you."

She tipped closer. "Because the buzz made him afraid he'd become a *beeeast*."

"Now you've done it," I said.

"Done what?" she said, tipping impossibly closer.

"Now you've made me break my rule about PDA." I picked her up and kissed her, only stopping with reluctance because I knew we were a spectacle and there were kids nearby.

"What happens now?" she asked, as breathless as I felt.

"Now we find our companions and go dancing," I said and squinted at her. "Can he dance?"

She shook her head. "There's only one man who can dance in my world, and I'm currently in his arms."

I gave an exaggerated sigh and set her down. "Fine, first I'll teach him to change a tire, then I'll teach him to dance. But I'm not going to teach him everything I know."

"Huntley, you could teach him everything you've ever learned, and it wouldn't make a difference because there is only one you, and you are mine, and I love you." She rested her head against me as I slid my arm around her, the feeling of *belonging* easing through me as I leaned down and kissed the top of her head, pausing to inhale her perfect Bellamy scent. *Home.*

It was hard to walk, anchored together as we were. I let go of her shoulders and took her hand, weaving our fingers together. "Bellamy, guess what?"

"What?" she asked, preemptively amused.

"You beeelong to me." I brought her hand to my lips and gave it a kiss as Michelle and Dylan trundled up to us.

Michelle huffed. "Are we still in the making out phase of things?"

"No," I said, facing them as I reached for my phone. "Let's call Lottie and Parker." Overflowing with love, I wanted all my available people near me right now.

"What are we going to do?" Michelle asked, trying to tamp down the hope and excitement in her tone. It was always thus with her, she was so afraid to be excited, so afraid to want something. It made me sad, so my words were a little somber as I spoke.

"Now we dance."

Michelle bit her lip uncertainly and looked to Bellamy, who nodded her agreement and reached out, clasping Michelle's hand in an enthusiastic grasp. "Now we dance," she agreed.

Michelle's gaze bounced back and forth between us. "Why do I feel like I'm about to enter a cult?"

"No," Bellamy said, now linking their arms together. "It's just the Mulligan way—it oozes light and joy to all it touches, like the sun."

I thought of my mom and dad then, of how hard they'd worked to give us a better life than what they'd had, and while they succeeded on a grander scale than they ever imagined, I thought maybe this might be the biggest benefit, that those around us who needed it could become Mulligans too, however peripherally. And someday when Bellamy and I had kids, I wanted it to continue, to eke joy and love and goodness to everyone we encountered. So I let go of Bellamy and forced myself to smile at a sullen Dylan as I started to roll my sleeves. "It's the Mulligan way," I agreed. "But first we change a tire."

As we walked outside the sun was setting, creating the perfect backdrop as I taught Dylan—and Bellamy and Michelle—how to change a tire. Next we moved on to the club, where Parker and Lottie met us, along with Sutton and Haven, who showed up a few days before their spring break to surprise me. We laughed and danced and talked and danced, and I don't think I've ever felt happier or more overflowing with every good thing. The best part? I knew for certain it would only get better, for both Bellamy and me.

Thank you for reading *Homeschool Huntley's First True Romance*, the second book in the Mulligans Series. For more books, please check out my website at www.vanessagraybartal.com.

www.ingramcontent.com/pod-product-compliance
Lightning Source LLC
Chambersburg PA
CBHW031236210726
48287CB00003B/800